Moon Curser

Ron Mueller

Moon Curser

Ron Mueller

Moon Curser
By: *Ron Mueller*

Around the World Publishing LLC
4914 Cooper Road Suite 144
Cincinnati, Ohio 45242-9998

This story is a work of fiction. Names, characters, places, and incidents either are products of the author's imagination or are used fictitiously. Any resemblance to actual events or locales or persons, living or dead, is entirely coincidental.

Moon Curser, Copyright © 2023

All rights reserved, including the right of reproduction, in whole or in part in any form.

ISBN 13: 978-1-68223-988-9
ISBN 10: 1-68223-988-8

Distributed by Ingram
Cover Picture by: AstroStar@ShutterStock
Cover Design by: Ron Mueller

Ron Mueller

Table of Content

Ron Mueller

<u>Chapter 1: Hidden Rise</u>

The Maite's cleaning van slowly approached the US-Mexican border crossing. Six people were laying in a false bottom chamber below the cleaning van bed. They were scared, silent and praying silently. The driver and her partner sitting on the other side shared a chocolate bag filled basket that lay between them.

The guards approached the familiar van and chatted with each of them. They handed each of the guards a small box of Swiss chocolate. This was an almost normal daily interaction that made it possible for the van to smuggle goods both ways. It smuggled a variety of goods or as in this case people got smuggled into the US and on the reverse trip it was beauty care products and other goods that got smuggled into Mexico.

The company was named after its founder Maite Manuela Flores who had single handedly started the company using an old car that she owned. Now, many years later and many such trips she was a person of tremendous wealth.

Maite was looking to buy another home. She had come to look at this home because it was only a short distance from Merida in the Yucatan where she had been born.

Her parents had both been working class people. They had legally emigrated to the United States when she was twelve and settled in Laredo, Texas.

Her mother had worked a variety of jobs and spent most of her working life as a cleaning lady in a large hotel.

Her father had gone through a series of jobs and felt lucky when he got a machinist job on the airbase because it provided him and the family with great benefits.

The two of them had been good parents. They supported her in school and as she neared high school graduation, they had encouraged her to go to college.

She had taken courses in business management, then toward the end she realized that she disliked but gritted her teeth and got her degree. She graduated near the bottom of her class. She had found most of the course work to be tedious and boring.

She found partying with her college friends much more to her liking. She also found out that she had little tolerance for the young men who were constantly trying to get her out on dates. Her opinion of the young women on the college campus was not much higher. This made her a loner that attended many parties as a single person.

Once she graduated, she took an office job but found it exceedingly dull and soon she was ready for something else.

Moon Curser

She was well versed in what her mother did because she had often accompanied her when she was younger. She decided that she would open a cleaning service. She started the business using her old car. The business soon grew, and she moved the business into a small secondhand van. Her approach of keeping the cost low and the cleaning approach efficient paid off and soon she was expanding her business. She named it Maite's Cleaners and had a smiling young woman painted on each side of her new larger white van.

Things seemed to dramatically improve when she expanded her business across the border into Nuevo Laredo. Business there was much better than she had expected. She was able to buy a larger full-sized step van as her second vehicle. She could not remember exactly how she started smuggling but she put the start when she bought several pairs of jeans for herself and then sold a few to some acquaintances at a significant profit. This experience opened a new way of thinking about how to run her business.

Cleaning provided a legitimate reason for her trucks entering Mexico and returning to the US. Smuggling soon provided the main income for the business.

She had personally installed a false bottom in the cleaning van. She had to learn to cut metal, to weld and then to raise the bed of her van so she could position and bolt in the false bottom.

The process had been something that had her learning new skills and one that she had enjoyed doing. It was such an easy modification and worked so well that she then envisioned having a fleet of cleaning trucks with the same alteration.

She made friends with the border guards on both sides of the border and provided them with small personal treats and gifts. They would see her, greet her, accept their gifts that were usually candy but if she knew of a birthday, she would add some small personal gift. They always then waved for her to pass.

She thought of the story of Ivan Petrovich Pavlov the Russian experimental neurologist and physiologist known for his discovery of classical conditioning through his experiments with dogs. She found that his theory worked exceedingly well with the border guards on both sides of the border.

The smuggling went very well and soon she expanded her operation. She grew by about one van every six months.

During the expansion period she seemed to spend most of her time bending metal, raising truck beds, and installing false bottoms.

She made a point of traveling with each of her new cleaning women or men long enough that they were all known to the guards on both sides of the boarder. She introduced them to the border guards and instructed her new hires to make sure to have treats and small gifts for the border guards each time they crossed.

Her crews were all selected based on their willingness to participate in the smuggling operation. They all eagerly went along when she offered ten percent of the money made which they would then split evenly.

She limited human smuggling driving to a few very trusted cleaning crews. They each received ten percent of a much higher dollar value and they were very loyal to her.

Maite knew that ten percent did not sound like much but for most of her workers, what they made working for her was about ten times more than they could make working anywhere else.

Her fortune seemed to grow exponentially. She made sure that the money that she accumulated was managed by professional money managers and that they designed an aggressive investment portfolio. She was willing to take a high risk. She was already doing that with her business.

She had opened four offshore bank accounts on four different Caribbean islands. It was a great way to vacation and to expand her money empire. She learned to move her money in small increments into the banks. She paid no taxes on the money that went to these banks. She figured she was making some thirty percent more on each dollar she put into those accounts.

She had become a Cayote by accident. One day she was at a party in Nuevo Laredo, where she was approached by the wife of one of the cartel leaders and was asked to meet with her husband. She was led to a private room where she was asked if she could transport six people into the US.

She was surprised at the invitation and the thoughtful approach that was taken in making the request. It was clear to her that this person knew about her smuggling business. She was impressed by the sum of money that was to be paid to her. She decided to try it and agreed to do it.

On the first trip she personally drove the cleaning van. She had made sure that the false bottom was clean and that the people she was transporting would be comfortable. She had provided each with a blanket to lay on and a pillow to rest their heads.

She then checked when the inspection agents that she felt would be the easiest to interact with were on duty and picked that day to make her first trip.

She instructed the six people she was transporting to be very quiet during the trip.

She had been very nervous on that first trip. She had her small gifts that she gave to the border guards, and she crossed over successfully. The trip went off with great success and the money she made convinced her that it was a business that was very worthwhile getting into.

At the next party where she had been approached with the request to take people across the border, she brought some very expensive cosmetics for the wife and a personalized wallet for her husband. These small gifts resulted in her getting invitations from several of the other major cartel leaders.

She made friends with many of the wives she met and always made the point that she was not in competition with any of the husbands but that she offered them a service that they could take advantage of when they needed it.

Her coyote business just kept growing. She got the people who were the cream of the Cayote traffic. These were people that had money up front to pay for the trip.

She recognized that she was prospering in the shadows of powerful cartels by being friendly and not personally seeking out people to smuggle.

She had built a very successful smuggling business empire. She was not into drugs and operated a low-key smuggling operation in the shadow of the drug cartels. Her main operation consisted of moving a significant quantity of blue jeans, furniture and periodically people across the border from Mexico into the US. She realized it was significant for her but almost insignificant to the amounts that the cartels smuggled into the US.

She was on good terms with several of the drug cartels because she knew the wives and the daughters of many of the cartel leaders. She supplied them with clothes and beauty products, and they influenced their husbands.

She had also buttered up several of the border guard teams on both sides of the border and she scheduled the crossing of her cleaning and laundry vehicles to coincide with their schedules.

Each of her trucks had a false bottom that could hold up to six people in a prone position. She most often used it to move clothing and furniture from Mexico into the US. Periodically she would smuggle people, but she preferred not to do it too often, so she charged a very high price. It seemed that this high price made her business more attractive to those that had more money.

She had started with one cleaning truck and had done all the work herself. She now had more than a dozen trucks, drivers and helpers.

She was not into gun play, but she now had two bodyguards that accompanied her almost everywhere.

She focused on managing the cash flow and expanding her holdings to include the legitimate making of the furniture and the making of the blue jeans. She had just acquired three furniture production and two blue jean production facilities. The cash flow from them was almost as significant as the smuggling side of the business because she was shipping goods south into south America, to the Asian market as well as into the US. The legal flow of goods was lucrative because her factory workers earned so little.

The smuggling side was still very attractive because though the amount was significantly less than the legitimate businesses, the margin on the smuggled goods was very high.

She had now been in business for many years. She had accumulated a very large sum of money, and she was no longer doing any hands-on work.

She was now looking at retiring and had found a potential house near her birthplace on the Yucatan peninsula.

She was now there and had walked through the three-story mansion during the day and was now making sure she liked it at night. Her realtor had been surprised at her request for a night walk through. He had smiled and said that it would be no problem and had asked what time she wanted to do the night walk through.

Standing and looking out of the second-floor veranda at the bright full moon's glittering reflection off the dark waters of the Gulf of Mexico convinced her that this would be her retirement home. It was not her home yet but soon would be. She had loved the view out to the gulf during the day and now she knew that it was even more to her liking at night.

She had been surprised when they had driven in for the night viewing. The lighted grounds were too ostentatious. They had put her off as they drove up the long lane to the house. She would have much lower-level lighting replace the glaring ones that made the area seem brighter than in the day. She certainly would not have them mounted in the trees and the palms. She felt that the lighting was offensive.

She reacted to the furniture in the house that she found offensive as well. She wondered about the people who had lived in the place. She hoped they planned to take the furniture with them.

The Kitchen area was another place that disappointed her. It was a well-planned kitchen layout but except for the hooded gas stove the rest of the appliances would all need to be replaced.

All these factors affected what she was willing to offer for the house. She felt the asking price was just too high. The realtor must not know the market or perhaps the people that could afford a multi-million-dollar waterfront home did not pay attention to the market. She offered seventy percent of the asking price with a certainty that she would end up getting it at about the eighty percent of the asking price.

When she gave her offer to the realtor, he shook his head and said that his client would not accept such a low offer. He had suggested an offer around ninety-five percent of the asking price.

She responded that she knew that the property had already been on the market for six months and had not sold. She commented that the payment could be arranged to be in cash if that would make the sale more attractive.

He responded that cash might be of interest.

Maite liked the possibility of paying in cash because it would help her move her money in a manner that allowed her to mix the profits from her legitimate businesses with the cash from her smuggling business.

Two days later when he came with the counteroffer, the realtor found her lazing on the beach in front of the home that she planned to buy.

Her two bodyguards were sitting under umbrellas located about fifty feet to each side of where she was laying. They both came over and checked the realtor out before letting him approach her.

The realtor shared the owner's counteroffer of seventy five percent of the asking price if the payment was in cash.

She arranged to have all the paperwork sent to her lawyer and when he cleared the property, the cash would be transferred to the bank of the seller's choosing.

Not long after the sellers responded that they would like the cash to be personally given to them versus going to a bank and they wanted it in US dollars.

Maite knew then that the sellers were trying to get their hands on the cash and never be held accountable to pay any taxes. She responded that they would need to personally pick up the cash at her Mexican lawyer's office in Mexico City. She figured they would most likely leave Mexico on a private boat and take the money to one of the islands.

She let them know that they would need to personally pick up the money at her lawyer's office. She made the point that the amount that they were requesting would take a truck to transport and they needed to arrange for that to happen.

The realtor asked if he could get his commission separately.

Maite replied that he should work that out with his client. She smiled and added that he should make sure he got his money before the money was loaded into the truck that was to transport his clients' money.

After the realtor left, she placed a call to her lawyer and explained what was happening and that he should arrange for the money to be brought to his office. This was money that Maite had that was being held in various personal vaults and had not seen the inside of a bank for some time. Now she would not have to move it into various offshore accounts to launder it. It would allow for new money to fill those various vaults.

She called each of the people that held the cash to let them know to send it to the lawyer. The five legal businesses held much of the cash but by moving it, the accountants could take a series of losses and the money would disappear from the books. That represented a significant gain.

The smuggling business had cash held in a variety of safes that would benefit by having them emptied so they could be refilled. That cash coming from all locations slowly filled the entire lawyers' meeting room.

The cash for the house was a significant transaction that would be a bump in the cash flow and would take a few months to level out. It might mean that she would take on smuggling more people for a short period of time.

She would work that out once she was back at her condominium in the US. She decided it was time to return to the where she owned an entire floor of a Beach Front condominium on Mustang Island. She was not planning to move out of the condominium and would retain it for the times she would be in the US.

Before she could move into her new home, she needed some time to buy the furniture, appliances, and light fixtures for the house.

She had taken the time to walk through her new home and had taken a picture of each room so she could work with her decorator to modernize the decor of her new home. She arranged to have her decorator that had done her condominium travel to her new home in the Yucatan and get a firsthand look at the house and then manage the transformation.

She planned to follow her old formula of a slow and steady approach that had served her well. She planned to continue doing what had worked for her over many years.

Other than causing a slight disruption in the cash flow, the cost of the house that she was now buying was insignificant compared to the money she held in various offshore accounts. She smiled as she thought how lucrative her smuggling shadow business continued to be. She had risen from a one-person operation to the point that she was now worth more than three billion dollars. She laughed when she realized that she was not sure what her true wealth was.

She would have been surprised to have known that there was someone finding out what that true wealth happened to be and where it was being held. In fact, she would be shocked when her wealth put her in the bull's eye of a person who would pursue her for the illicit way, she had accumulated her money.

She had no way of knowing that she would be answering for all her past actions that she had taken in the shadows of the society that she had flourished in as she took advantage of her ability to skirt the law.

<u>Chapter 2: Shadow Hunters</u>

Brian and Kekoa were sitting side by side in their common first floor veranda work area that was used more often than the more formal second floor office. The panoramic view across the waters to Lanai's mixed green and tan landscape, the mountain top wind turbines on the ridge to the west, the view of Kahoolawe that had once been used as a target range by the US Navy and the small Molokini Crater that looked like a broke tooth sticking up above the water was augmented by the warm sun and a pleasant breeze that was wafting across the veranda.

Each of them was nursing a lemonade and talking back and forth. They agreed that work didn't get any better than what they were doing. Together they were studying the number of billionaires that existed just in the US. Most of these billionaires were above-board individuals that seemed to populate every profession. Kekoa commented that he had never imagined so many people having so much money.

Brian said that he too was surprised at the number of billionaires but added that they represented less than one per cent of the population. He then made the point that they were looking for the ones that were hiding in the shadows at the edge of or on the other side of the law. He shared how he had proceeded with the two billionaires that he had successfully put behind bars. Those individuals had operated on the edge of the law with one foot on each side of the line.

Kekoa shook his head and said that he needed to figure out what he personally had been doing wrong because it seemed that some of the billionaires had stumbled into their extreme wealth. He wanted to figure out how to stumble in the same way.

Brian nodded and added that the entertainment industry seemed to be churning out most of the new billionaires and many of the others had inherited their wealth and were from older money lines.

He added that they needed to find someone who was complaining about bad treatment from some wealthy individuals or who felt wronged by one. The ones in the shadows would most likely be the ones that did not make the news and who were quietly going about making their illicit money by taking advantage of someone or some group of less wealthy people.

He suggested they look at the news reporting on local issues along the Mexican-US border and along the Canadian-US border. Other places might be in the housing markets around the larger cities.

Kekoa made a list of the cities they should check. The list included, San Diego-Tijuana, El Paso-Ciudad Juarez, Laredo-Nuevo Laredo, Hidalgo-Reynosa, Brownsville-Matamoros.

He pointed out that the five paired cities were cities on each side of the border across from each other.

Brian commented that he thought they would be working for a while through news reports trying to find the billionaire needle in the haystack. He wondered if there was a way to speed up the process.

Kekoa suggested putting together a computer driven routine based on key words to filter the news reports and get the number of reports reduced to a handful for each city pair. He said he had an idea how to do that and it would only take a few moments. He suggested that the two of them work together to make a list of key search words.

A week later Brian commented that the routine had reduced the number, but his estimate of a week was going to go longer than he had expected. He added that there was more misery to sort through than he had anticipated.

Kekoa commented that he had found an interesting and peculiar court case where a young illegal Mexican migrant claimed to have been smuggled in by a cleaning company and then abandoned when she complained about having spent so much time confined in the dark compartment of a truck and getting her only outfit covered in grease. She had paid her family's life savings to make the trip and had expected better treatment. She however did not give any specific details and was scheduled to be sent back to Mexico.

Brian asked where she was currently being held.

Kekoa said that currently she was being held in Laredo.

Brian said he thought that it was a case they should examine more closely. He said that he was going to see if he could meet in person with her and find out about the smuggling operation. He commented that whoever was running the operation stood to make a lot of money. He just hoped that the smuggler that had brought her across was not directly connected to one of the cartels.

He let out a groan when he realized that it was more than an eight-hour trip with one stop and layover on the way. In addition to flying, he would have to drive from San Antonio to Laredo. That was the best flight, and a seat was available that evening. He decided to book the flight and make it as quick a trip as possible.

He let Kekoa know that they should stay connected even as he flew and that he should continue to find out more if he could.

The flight turned out to be just as grueling as he had anticipated. He got some sleep along the way and after arriving in Houston he went out for a good breakfast and several cups of coffee. He then made the three-hour drive from San Antonio to Laredo.

Kekoa had provided him the address where the young lady was still being held. He decided to go straight there when he drove into Laredo.

He figured that he was cutting it really close since her deportation hearing was to take place the next day.

Once he was in the building where she was being held, he inquired if there was any other alternative to her deportation. He was informed that a US citizen would need to step forward to sponsor her and that so far none had done that. He thanked the receptionist for the information and arranged for the interview.

She was twenty-two years old, five foot two inches tall and petite. Her name was Carmen Torres. She was wearing an orange jump suit when she was escorted into the interview room with a confused look on her face.

She started to speak in Spanish, so Brian smiled and answered her in his native Hawaiian.

She smiled and in English asked what language he had been speaking.

He let her know that he was raised as a Hawaiian and that he knew the native Hawaiian, English, and only knew how to order a beer in Spanish.

She grinned and said how to order a beer were the first words she had learned in English.

Brian liked her attitude. It was clear to him that she was confused and scared but she was resilient.

He then let her know that he was interested in her case and what she knew about the group or persons that had smuggled her into the US. He let her know that he had all the information that had been taken by the border agents. He added that what he was interested in was for her to describe how she had gotten connected to the smuggling group, what she had experienced, who and what she had seen. Perhaps she might remember something that she had so far not thought of as important.

Carmen closed her eyes, was silent for a long time then she said that the only thing that came to mind that she had not already shared with the people that had interrogated her was that she had been introduced to the smuggler leader through a friend that was the daughter of one of the cartel minor chiefs. The smuggler was wearing a cleaning lady's outfit with the name Maite's Cleaners on the shoulder of her blouse.

Brian knew that he had just hit pay dirt.

He raised his hand and stopped her for a moment. He then made a call to Kekoa and asked him to dig into Maite's Cleaners and see what he could learn.

He then turned his attention back to Carmen and asked her to share her personal background and experience. He found out that she had attended a hotel management and catering school in Nuevo Loredo and had hoped to make the US her home, get a job and send money home to help her family. She gave a small laugh and said she could have crossed as a tourist and have never gone back but decided to get into the country via being smuggled so that she would not be searched for.

He asked her if she were willing to work for one of the Hotels in Hawaii.

Carmen teared up and began crying.

Brian knew he had hit a nerve and was silent for a moment. He handed her his clean handkerchief.

She took it and asked if he could possibly arrange such a thing.

He asked the attending border control officer and asked what he had to do to sponsor Carmen.

After a call, another person entered the room and asked for his passport, his job status, and if he would cover Carmen's living expenses. He would also need to show that he had sufficient funds in his bank to do so.

He provided her with the information.

She said that she would process the paperwork but that it would take the rest of the afternoon. She would make a copy of his credentials and return them in a few moments but then the rest of the paperwork would not be ready until the morning. She said she was aware that they were cutting it very close because Carmens case was scheduled just before lunch.

He asked whether Carmen would be able to leave with him and was told that if Carmen agreed then the two of them could leave but she had to return the next morning with him to sign some papers as well.

He then asked if she had more than the orange jumpsuit and learned that her clothes had been ruined by grease. They had been washed but would have stains on them.

Carmen said that an orange jump suit was not very practical out in public and that she would prefer to wear her grease-covered clothes.

The guard suggested they return to her holding cell, and she would bring her clothes to her.

He looked at Carmen and in Hawaiian said, "E ʻike iā ʻoe i hoʻokahi minute."

Carmen smiled and replied, "Estoy deseando que llegue, (I am looking forward to it), Estoy tan emocionada, (I am so excited.)" She did not know exactly what he had said but figured it was something like, "see you in a few.

Carmen was taken back to the holding area and allowed to change. She was led out to the lobby where Bryan was sitting.

Brian took in the pair of jeans that had a black streak across the legs and a similar streak went across the front of her light blue blouse.

He asked her if she had all her personal possessions and she said that she originally had one hundred dollars in cash and a bracelet in a small black leather belt pouch.

Brian asked the escort where they could retrieve the rest of Carmen's possessions. She led them to a person sitting behind a caged in area. There Carmen gave her name and described the pouch and its contents.

The attendant went to a back room and came out with the pouch, opened it, and displayed the money and the bracelet.

Carmen picked up the pouch, put her bracelet on and put the money back into the pouch. She thanked the attendant and turned and followed Brian.

He led the way out of the building and after getting oriented led the way to his rental car.

He let her know that he was first going to get her registered in the same hotel that he was in and then they would go shopping for several sets of clothes for her.

On the way to the Hotel, he received a call from Kekoa. He answered briefly but said he would call him back in a few.

The hotel had only one deluxe room with a king-sized bed left. Brian said he would take it.

He handed the key cards to Carmen and suggested that they first go shopping and afterwards get lunch and then return to the hotel.

Carmen pointed out that she did not have much money and that shopping would need to be minimal.

Brian smiled and said that he was going to show Carmen a way to stretch her money while she still got all of what she needed. He took a moment, located a used clothes store, and drove there.

He watched as Carmen went slowly looking through a series of clothes.

He sat down in one of the chairs that were for sale and made a call to Kekoa. He listened as his excited partner said that they had hit pay dirt. He said that Maite's Cleaners was owned by one Maite Manuela Flores who had a large sum of money in a bank in Corpus Christy, Texas and offshore accounts in Haiti, St. Lucia, Barbados, and Jamaica. The total amount in those banks exceeded three billion and Maite also owned several factories in Mexico that would add to her total wealth. So, Carmen's simple recollection had opened the door to the pursuit of the next billionaire. He added that Maite seemed to be operating with the consent of various cartels.

Brian decided that Carmen would begin her new life journey with a part of any reward that he and Kekoa received.

He and Kekoa had recently agreed to a fifty, fifty split. He would take five percent of his split and give it to Carmen.

He figured that it would change her life when she came into a few million dollars. He figured that he would wait until that money was truly in hand before saying anything.

Carmen had selected a black pant suit, a lavender pant suit, a pair of jeans, a sport blouse, a pair of black flat shoes, a pair of high-heeled shoes and a black leather purse. When they got to the check out the final bill came to seventy-two dollars and sixty-five cents.

Carmen was beaming as she held up her purchase. She had tears in her eyes and gave Brian a hug.

She asked if they could stop at a Target or similar store so she could spend her last few dollars on some additional things that she wanted to buy.

A short drive later, Brian handed her five twenties as they walked in and said that it was a loan until she had a job.

She gave him another hug and thanked him.

On the way to lunch Carmen asked what kind of job he was in that allowed him to sponsor her, had the money to put her up in a top-end hotel, pay for her airfare to Hawaii and give her money to spend.

Brian smiled and said that he was not sure what his work title should be, but he was in the business of putting cheating billionaires in front of a judge and jury. And then hope to see a verdict that corresponded to their cheating behavior.

Carmen was silent for a moment and asked who paid him to do that.

He smiled, shook his head, and said the billionaires paid him royally. He had only had two previous experiences in dealing with wayward billionaires and he was still waiting for the reward money from the IRS for the second billionaire he had fingered for them. His first billionaire had put nineteen million dollars into his pocket. The reward for the second billionaire would be likely be close to ninety million dollars. The billionaire that Carmen had surfaced would most likely be significantly more.

Carmen shook her head and said that she had never thought about a bounty hunter that went after billionaires. She commented that she was really interested in how such a business worked. It seemed to her that it could also be a very dangerous affair. She shook her head and said that a billionaire had lots of money to use to protect themselves.

Brian nodded and said that he had thought a lot about that angle of chasing down wayward billionaires and was taking the actions he hoped would keep him alive to continue to pursue his odd career.

<u>Chapter 3: Connection</u>

On his return to Maui, Brian took Carmen to the hotel directly in front of his home and got her checked in. He suggested that she take advantage of the hotel's restaurants and the many guest activities. He gave her two hundred dollars in cash and suggested she also take in the shops and other eating venues that were in the area. He let her know that he or someone else would periodically check on how she was doing. He gave her his phone number and told her to call if she needed any help.

He knew that Annie had arrived the day before. When he walked into the house, she greeted him with a hug and kiss. He was overjoyed to see her. They were a few weeks away from her and the two girls moving permanently to Maui. He was looking forward to that day when the whole family would be together. He and Annie had shuttled back and forth between Maui and Cincinnati and agreed that it always threw their body clock off.

Annie teased him about running around with a girl almost half of his age.

He smiled and answered that it was only because the girl was so good-looking that he could not help himself. He then added that she had also pointed his efforts at the next billionaire that he and Kekoa were now pursuing.

Annie said that made her feel much better that it was the money he was after and gave him another hug and kiss.

He had the same reaction that he had when she had given him her first kiss. This time he took her in his arms and carried her into the bedroom.

Later during lunch, he made the point that he was likely going to make about another ninety million. He planned to reward Carmen with five percent of that or around four million dollars. He wondered if perhaps Annie could coach Carmen so that she would be ready for such an influx of money.

Annie smiled and said that it had been hard for her to absorb the wealth that had suddenly come her way when she was rescued, but she had two young children that gave her a different perspective of what she should do with her newfound wealth. She also had the coaching of Alex, the person who had rescued her and who had recognized the value of the fifteen years of paintings that she had generated during the fifteen years she was chained in the cabin in the forests of Pennsylvania. She also had Alex's work partner's wife whose son was now the girl's best friend. Finally, she had her parents who helped her get readjusted into a tremendously changed society.

She said that she had needed all the support that had come her way because she had to overcome her own mental problems in getting used to being free and making her own decisions.

She commented that Carmen needed her help, but she also needed to make new friends of her own age and get into the great social scene that existed on Maui.

She would see how she might help Carmen. She asked when the money might come in for her.

Brian replied that the timing would depend on how quickly the case that he was now working on could be closed and the reward allocated. He figured it would be several years.

Annie asked whether they should be concerned about the fact that this person that he was after was operating on the illegal side of the law and was involved in smuggling people out of Mexico into the US. She made the point that such a person was most likely connected with some drug cartel. She might also be willing to engage violently if she felt threatened.

Brian nodded and said that he had taken Alex's suggestion that he become proficient with a gun. He added that he and Kekoa were both going to the gun range twice a week and practicing with their new high-end, three-fifty-seven, six shot revolvers that were rated top in the field. He added that he had purchased the weapon that Alex had suggested and was following her guidance and getting her advice on how to improve his aim. He had qualified as a marksman first level and was pursuing getting to the top level; level five.

He went over to the cabinet in the living room and brought out his revolver. It was black, had a scope mounted on it and had the grip molded to fit his hand. He also had a silencer that made the gun look like a small cannon.

Annie commented that it was a good-looking weapon and much more elaborate than the one that she knew Alex carried.

Brian reiterated the fact that he and Kekoa had bought the weapon based on Alex's recommendation.

He then showed her the full Kevlar outfit that Alex had also recommended. He added that he planned to follow Alex's advice to always wear the jacket when out in the field.

Annie smiled and said she felt much better knowing that he was getting coaching from Alex. She went on to say that it seemed that he and Alex had bonded, and that Alex was providing much needed guidance to a soft loveable guy that she had fallen in love with.

Brian said that he was learning about many of Alex's cases and was amazed at what she had done in the short time she had been in the field.

Annie nodded and said that she was amazed at how much money he had made in the short time that he was in the field and that it seemed to her that he had focused his efforts on the top of the money-making ladder.

Brian shook his head and replied that it was not about the money but about finding those at the very top that seemed determined to step on the backs of those at the bottom to make their fortune. He had not realized how much money he stood to make until he went through the first two cases. In those cases, he had focused on making sure those who had been cheated out of their money received most of the settlement.

He commented that he was not sure how he was going to handle any monies that he recouped on this round. Except for Carmen, it seemed that he would not be able to directly aid those who had been cheated.

He then commented that he was going to contact Harold Zimmerman, the Chicago DEA unit leader that Alex had recommended. He was seeking his advice on how he should proceed to get his current target in front of a US judge versus one in Mexico. He added that if any of the cartels were involved the person he was after would most likely get off and never make it into a Mexican court.

Annie said that after lunch she was going to set up her painting set in the veranda by the pool and do another Maui scenic painting. She asked what he was going to do.

Brian said that he and Kekoa were scheduled for a two o'clock time slot on the firing range. He hoped to step up to the next marksmanship level during this session.

He smiled and said that when he qualified at level five, he was going to try Alex's feat of putting six shots dead center of the target while being blindfolded.

Annie gave him a hug and said she did not know how Alex had ever been able to do it and she would continue to love him even if he could not do such a thing.

He realized that his call to Harold would need to wait until the next morning and decided to put his full attention to improving his gun handling skills. He once again cleaned his already clean weapon in preparation of going to the gun range.

Once at the range, Kekoa and he practiced continually for an hour. They both had improved significantly since the time that they had started. The Range Master complimented them as he qualified them at the next level up.

Leilani had come into the gun range for her own practice time and had watched them for their last ten minutes of practice and complemented both for the significant improvement they had made. She examined their choice of weapon and commented that they had chosen a top-of-the-line weapon and added that she was jealous, but she had learned from Alex that it was not the gun but the hand, the eye and the smooth trigger finger pull that made the bullet find the bull's eye. And it was the practice, practice, practice, at the range and envisioning the real gun fight that made a difference in the field.

Kekoa nodded and said that he had never imagined owning a gun and he found it strange that he liked coming to the firing range to use it. He, however, could not imagine being in a gun fight.

Leilani agreed and then added that it had been when she witnessed Alex shoot the person who was about to cut someone's throat that had made her want to improve her skill. Alex's shot had to miss the victim by less than an inch. The realization of the skill and confidence needed to take that shot led her to religiously make two weekly visits to the firing range.

She added that the person saved that day by Alex was now a detective in Oahu. Before being saved she had been a heavy drinker but had gone cold turkey when she realized that it was that habit that had almost led to her death.

Brian smiled and added that he inspired by Alex and that he was learning a ton from her. She had a way of coaching that seemed natural and personalized to what a person needed.

Leilani agreed and added that she had also learned to be a more nurturing and developmental boss from her. It had changed how she and everyone in the Maui police department worked with each other. It had made work more fun, and everyone seemed to experience less stress.

Leilani pointed at the clock and said she had to get to her position and do her hour of practice.

Kekoa had been quietly listening. He said that he was changing the subject and asked if Brian had anything special planned for dinner.

Brian asked what he might have in mind.

Kekoa said that they could take Annie out to their favorite outdoor restaurant and have a round of beers and then dig into some tacos and perhaps a good helping of surf and turf with onion rings on the side.

Brian made a quick call to Annie who said that a dinner out fit her current mood if they did not stay out too late.

Brian agreed and said that he was still suffering from jet lag and would welcome a good night's sleep.

Dinner turned out to be a quiet three-person affair. The order had been more than they could consume but Kekoa took the extra food home with him.

Brian and Annie returned home and turned in early.

The next morning after a hearty breakfast, he placed the call to Harold. Their discussion was fruitful. Harold suggested that, if possible, the arrest should occur in the US. If that were the case, he would make sure that the DEA would provide support. If the situation were to take place in Mexico, the goal would be to bring the subject back into the US if possible. Harold gave Brian the number to an Eduardo Gomez that had a similar role in Mexico to a DEA agent in the US. He said that he and Eduardo went back quiet a few years and had facilitated getting the bad guy in front of the right legal entity which was usually in the US.

Moon Curser

After the discussion with Harold, Brian gave Eduardo a call. He introduced himself and shared that Harold had suggested they talk. He described the case that he was building against a Maite Manuela Flores a naturalized American citizen that also claimed Mexican citizenship. He made the point that she was carrying on an illegal smuggling operations across the US-Mexican border.

When he shared the name, Eduardo commented that he had never heard of the woman that they were discussing but that he would check around to see what he could find out.

Brian said that he had been surprised at the extreme wealth she had amassed while remaining invisible to the law enforcement agencies in two countries. He added that he was also surprised at the low-key approach that had made her successful in an environment that was extremely hostile to competition in the smuggling of goods and of ferrying fugitives across the border. He added that she also had several legitimate businesses that turned a significant profit, making furniture and in the manufacture of blue jeans under several brand names. By mixing the legitimate business cash flows with her illicitly obtained cash she could rather easily launder her money.

Eduardo said that he would take a closer look to see if he could find out more about this person because he too wondered how she kept herself out of the middle of all the fighting between cartels.

The fact that she ran some legitimate businesses impressed him since this was good for the country. It was clear to him that she was the yin and the yang of what went on in Mexico.

Brian let him know that he planned to visit Mexico during the coming week to go to see a sea-front home that she had just purchased in the Yucatan state. He asked if Eduardo might want to accompany him. The two could then strategize how to proceed against this individual.

Eduardo asked what she would be charged with. When he learned that the most likely charge would be tax evasion, he said that she should be arrested in the United States or be taken across the border if she was apprehended in Mexico. Eduardo added that in Mexico if she had the kind of money that Brian was alluding to, she would most likely be able to pay off the judge and get away Scot free.

He then added that he would like to participate with Brian. He could provide a car and driver and he could provide some fire power if it were needed.

The two of them agreed to the day and time on the following week when Brian would arrive in Mexico City.

Eduardo said that he would meet him, and they would then drive to the see the house together.

Chapter 4 Exposed

As far as the eye could see, the white caps appeared to be the snow-covered tops of mountains moving towards her. The grey clouds rolled lazily along carried by the warm summer air that carried the odor of salt with a tinge of the aroma of seaweed. She let it all flow over her and closed her eyes and listened to the waves as they reached the shore and seemed determined to slap the shoreline for its refusal to give way. This location had captured her the first time she had entered the condominium. Her walk along the beach had sealed her desire to purchase the condominium.

Maite enjoyed her Padre Island condominium. It was one of her several homes but the only one in the US. She was relaxing in her condominium veranda and enjoying nature display its angry mood.

She shortly absorbed and reflected the same mood as she had absorbed on the veranda. The angry mood was triggered by the call she received from her snitch informer that called to let her know that the young woman who had been arrested and detained after she had been smuggled into the US had been sponsored and whisked away by a person named Brian O'Neill.

He added that he was currently working with a friend at the airport trying to find out where they had gone.

She turned and entered the calm of her day room and decided to call her personal lawyer and asked him to see if he could learn more about the situation. She figured he could access the court proceedings and learn where Brian O'Neill lived.

She was personally worried that the person who had been whisked away might give away her smuggling operational secrets. She had never met this Carmen, but she might know more than she should. Maite had worked very hard to keep her smuggling operation low key and concealed. She did not want some disgruntled illegal border crosser screwing up her operation.

She was not usually a violent person and had tried very hard to stay clear of the many battles that were constantly in play in the Mexican cartel's relationships. This situation, however, caused her great concern. She was planning her retirement but wanted her operation to continue to enrich her. She realized that she was willing to eliminate both the person who could potentially expose her operation and the person who sponsorship had rescued her.

She alerted her two personal bodyguards about the situation and instructed them to keep an eye out for anyone that seemed too curious about her or her operation. She did the same with the persons running her legitimate operations as well as the person running the day-to-day smuggling operation.

She decided to carry through with her plans to go and enjoy her new Yucatan home as she had planned and flew there during the afternoon. The change in the weather to a sunny, lightly cloud spectacled day help improve her mood.

She went out and sat under an umbrella in her beach reclining chair. It was not long after that she received a call from an informant that worked out of Mexico City. He let her know about a Mexican DEA agent that had been looking into her manufacturing and clothe making operations.

This caused her to sit up and take a long drink of her spiked pink lemonade. She felt that she needed to take some sort of action but was not sure where to begin. She put in a call to her informant in El Paso and asked her to find out where the person named Carmen Torres had gone and to do it as quickly as possible. She figured it was time to begin to clear the back trail and eliminate the people that might be able to expose her. She figured that the time to be low key and non-confrontational was over. She was now ready to act and the actions she had in mind were not kind ones.

She decided to take a quick dip, then go in take a long shower, afterwards she would contact her second in charge of the smuggling operation and let him know that he should be very careful to cull the people currently asking to be transported into the US.

She figured that if the DEA found out about her migrant smuggling operation, they would try to plant an informant to document the smuggling process. She needed to prevent this at all costs.

The fact that one person could cause her a big problem had always been on her mind. She had always been vigilant about giving her migrant customers a positive experience and a positive release in the US. This had worked very well for all the years that she had run her cayote business. She shook her head as she thought about the fact that this Carmen had probably been treated very well but now, she needed to eliminate her as a potential threat if she were going to protect the business she had worked hard to build.

She wondered what this Brian person who had mysteriously appeared on the scene and whisked Carmen away was about and why he had taken Carmen under his wing.

Who was this mystery person?

Was he connected with the DEA?

What was his interest in the situation?

Was one of the cartels using him to get to her? She laughed at this last thought and figured no cartel would use that kind of finesse if they were after her. They would just send an assassin to take care of the situation.

She was bent on finding out who he was, and she was willing to spend whatever funds it took to eliminate him. She smiled as she thought about the fact that she had the money, and she was worth every penny she might need to spend to make sure she would keep it.

Brian sat sipping his iced tea and enjoying the morning Maui sunrise and the balmy morning breeze. He had no clue that he had become a person of interest to a potentially deadly enemy.

Kekoa had located the seaside home on the Yucatan where Maite had taken up residence. They had agreed that he should get a firsthand look at the home and perhaps get a better understanding of the situation.

They needed to understand their quarry better than they did currently.

Kekoa took Brian to the airport where he caught a direct flight to Mexico City.

When he landed, he was met by Eduardo as he cleared the security area.

After greetings, Eduardo suggested that they drive to Coatzacoalcos and enjoy the evening there. Then the next morning they would drive on to the Yucatan location and arrive early in the evening. He added that this would allow Brian to sit back during the drive and recover from the long flight.

He suggested that after the surveillance of Maite's property and layout they would retrace the route with a slight detour that would let him introduce Brian to a person that might be of help. He added that this person was very influential, with connections in the cartels and might provide additional information that the two of them might find hard to obtain.

Brian said that it sounded like a good itinerary, and he was ready to travel.

Eduardo introduced the limo driver as Ricardo. Ricardo in turn pointed out the comfortable reclining seats and highlighted the refreshments that were available. Brian was tired from his flight from Maui and dozed off for much of the trip. He thanked Eduardo for waking him up to show him some of the more impressive vistas of the Mexican countryside and the mountain pass views.

He took the time to snap a few pictures and sent them on to Annie, the girls and Kekoa.

Annie texted back that his trip was looking more like a vacation than a business trip.

He replied that it was grueling to sit, doze off, then awakened to see the beautiful sights along the way and sent a smiley Emoji.

Eduardo asked Brian about his family and learned that Annie was the love of his life, and the two girls were wonderful rewards that came with Annie. Eduardo nodded and said that family was very important. He emphasized that it was really the most important thing in one's life. He shared the fact that he had moved his family to the US where they could live in a safer environment. He remained in Mexico but traveled every other week to the US to see his family. This made him feel better but really put a strain on his ability to be active in the everyday affairs of his young children as they were growing up.

Brian nodded and said that he understood and hoped that Eduardo would be able to move his role into a similar role somewhere in the US so he could be with his family.

The next day they arrived at Maite's seaside residence. They followed a public beach access road that was lined by palm trees surrounded by thick dark green grass that almost looked like it was meant to be on a golf green. They parked the limo in the parking lot. Then he and Eduardo took a narrower path similarly lined with palms surrounded by the same dark green grass. The view ahead reminded Brian of the view of Molokini in Annie's painting that currently hung over the fireplace mantle. They walked casually along the beach towards Maite's house.

The incoming waves were gently rolling in and running along the beach towards them. Brian resisted taking off his shoes to walk barefoot along the edge of the waves. He was a few steps in the lead and was just commenting about the great view when, unexpectedly something hit him in the chest and caused him to stagger back. He reacted instinctively, pulled his weapon, and returned fire to a person that was standing up the beach holding his gun with two hands. His shot hit the shooter in the chest, and the shooter went down. Brian then knelt and looked through the small scope sight on his weapon and observed two people entering the house. He recognized Maite from the photo that Kekoa had given him. He figured the large male was another of the bodyguards.

He wondered why he had been shot. He and Eduardo had made no aggressive move. It was clear that Maite and her team were very nervous and he and Eduardo, dressed in suites, were not beach walkers. Brian figured that Maite had overreacted and told the fallen bodyguard to shoot the two intruders.

Eduardo had dropped to the ground when Brian had been shot but had not fired his own weapon. He jumped up and came over to Brian and asked where he had been hit.

Brian put his finger through his suit jacket to show where the bullet had entered. He then picked out the shattered, flattened lead bullet and handed it to Eduardo. He commented that he had not expected to be shot.

He wondered what had alarmed Maite enough to have her bodyguards shoot at them without warning.

Eduardo pulled back Brian's suit jacket and put his hand on the Kevlar vest. He said it was lucky that Brian had been wearing such a vest. He shook his head and said that he needed to invest in such a lifesaving vest.

Eduardo then added that perhaps the fact that he had been digging into her business dealings had reached her. He then commented that he had never seen anyone with such a quick reaction since the time he had watched Alex take down a wayward priest with her tiny pen knife. He then asked if Brian had a legal permit in Mexico to carry his weapon and was relieved when he learned that Brian had indeed properly registered his weapon.

Brian walked quickly to where the shooter had fallen. The large hole in the chest that was still oozing blood and the lack of breathing verified that the shooter was dead.

Eduardo commented that he was not going to go any further toward the house and that they should leave the site and leave the area as quickly as possible.

He asked whether Brian was feeling well enough to make a long drive to see an old friend that everyone referred to as the "Angel on the Hill."

Brian nodded and said he needed the help of an angel and that they should high tail it in case Maite had a local support group.

Brian opened his shirt to check his chest to see where he had been hit. He knew he was going to have a large bruise. He noted that the Kevlar vest had been what had saved him. It was another one of Alex's coaching points that had paid off. He figured he owned her big time for her advice and coaching.

Once in the car, he got on the phone and ordered some Gourmet Chocolate Bars from one of Cincinnati's famous shops and had them sent to her apartment with a message of "Thanks for the coaching. It saved my life."

The next day he received an Emoji smiley face, followed by two hands in prayer from her.

He soon fell asleep and only came awake when he heard Eduardo speaking to a person that was standing next to the car holding a machine gun. He watched the gate in front of the car as it slowly opened. It was dark but it seemed they were in a tunnel that focused on what seemed like a huge mansion, lights came on and the car stopped. He got out and was surrounded by a group of people that were immediately checking on his well-being.

It was clear to him that Eduardo had called ahead.

Eduardo was greeted by a very beautiful woman who he brought over and introduced as Angelica Calderon better known as "The Angel on the Hill."

Angelica gave him a hug and said that a friend had introduced her to hugging and she preferred it to shaking hands.

Brian smiled and said that he had the same friend and her advice had saved his life.

Anglica replied that she had also saved hers. She took his hand and led the way into the house.

Once they were inside, Angelica led the way into a grand office and had everyone sit at the table. She asked Brian for his suit jacket and then put her finger through the bullet hole and then held up the suit to the light and commented that the bullet had shattered and had the shattered parts had made Swiss cheese from the jacket and she figured the shirt might have the same problem. She shook her head and said that he had been hit by a hollow point bullet.

She then put her finger lightly on the spot on his chest that would be over the spot where the bullet had hit. She said that she would make sure that he had some pain-relieving salve brought to his room so he could put it on before going to sleep.

She had some wine poured for everyone and asked to hear what Brian and Eduardo had done to have someone shoot at them.

Brian described walking along the beach to get a view of Maite's house and commented that they had not expected the shooting.

Eduardo added that had he been in the lead he would most likely be dead. Brian had been the closest to the shooter, was the one that was hit and the one that returned fire and killed the shooter.

Brian said that their mistake was to be dressed in suits and be walking on a very empty beach.

She nodded and said that she had met Maite once at a benefit gathering that she had sponsored. At that time, she had accepted a generous gift to the charity from her. She added that she never checked where the money from donors came from. She accepted it and put it to use in her charity. She said that she would have her network look for more information about the lady.

She then asked why Brian and Eduardo were checking on Maite.

Brian let her know that he was pursuing her because she was involved in smuggling people into the US, and she was in his sites because she had amassed several billion dollars illegally and his passion in life was to have people like her brough in front of a judge and jury to account for their actions.

Angelica smiled and said that she hoped not to get in his sights because of the similar large sums of money she held in various accounts.

Brian raised his glass, shook his head, and declared a toast, "anyone referred to as 'The Angel on the Hill' will be exempt." He then said that he was ready for a long hot shower and a good night's sleep.

Chapter 5 The Chase

Maite was furious when she discovered that Mateo, one of her guards, was dead. He had been shot in the heart. She knew he was an excellent shot and had fired on the two people walking down the beach. It had been clear to her that the two were not beach goers since they were both wearing suits. She had not witnessed the shooting but the fact that one of the persons had returned a shot accurately enough to kill Mateo either made that person very lucky or the shooter was an excellent gunman. She really didn't care which was the case, she just wanted revenge.

She called her local police contact and asked him to take care of the situation and to keep it very low key. Then she asked whether he could get the Traffic Police to locate an out of state car.

She asked Pedro, her remaining bodyguard, if he was ready to chase down and eliminate the two that had killed Mateo.

Pedro commented that he would face the devil if it meant he had a chance to kill the two. He then led the way to the limo.

Maite decided that she would sit in front versus sitting in the back as she normally did. She wanted to sit close to Pedro as they pursued the two that had been on the beach.

She let Pedro speed but suggested he keep it down to the point that the Traffic Police would not stop them. She let him know that she would periodically get updates as to where the car they were after was going. It was a long drive, and by driving without stopping they managed to catch up and get into view of the black limo.

She was surprised when she saw the car turn up the lane to a home that she knew had belonged to the previous Gulf Cartel Leader. She had Pedro drive slowly by the end of the lane. She then told him to drive into San Luis Potosi. They stopped at one of the better hotels and found two rooms for the night. She made several calls to learn who now owed the estate and was surprised that it was the previous Gulf Cartel leader's wife who had turned the estate into a home for people in need.

She recalled donating money to her in a recent fund-raising event that had been sponsored by a very elegant looking woman who was referred to as "The Angel on the Hill." Now she knew what hill that angel lived on.

The fact that the car she had pursued had gone there did not escape her. The people in the car had a powerful connection and she would have to be careful.

She decided that it would be better for her to momentarily defer her revenge and carefully plan how she was going to deter any continued investigation of herself. She came to the decision that she was going to have to play a game of chess versus checkers.

The chess game that she had decided to play would lead her to Hawaii. She learned through her information network that Carmen Torres, the young lady that she had smuggled into the US, was now living in Maui.

She left Mexico and went to her beachside home on Padre Island, Texas. She spent a few days interviewing several hit men that acted as bodyguards. She picked one that had some good references and who could openly travel on a current US passport. Once he was in place and had moved into her home, she was ready to fly to Maui.

She kept telling herself that the trip was strictly an information gathering trip. Her anger at losing her previous bodyguard had been replaced with the goal of neutralizing whomever was poking into her personal life. She had some remorse for Mateo, but he had shot first at someone that had not actually initiated such action. She had arranged to use a beach front home owned by one of her Mexican cartel associates.

She flew to Honolulu on a private charter and then took a local charter to Maui. It was a little more expensive than flying a commercial flight, but it was significantly faster, and it let her be more invisible.

She would later be surprised that she was anything but invisible but instead had been tracked from her home to the house on Maui.

Kekoa and Brian were sharing their morning breakfast by the pool. They were discussing the purpose of Maite's travel to Maui. Brian put his hand on his chest where the hand sized bruise from the bullet impact was now a faint purple and yellow color and said that maybe she had come to finish the job that her bodyguard had failed to accomplish.

He complemented Kekoa at having been able to track her travel to Maui and in getting the rental car license plate number as she left the airport. He pointed down to the area where the car had gone along the beach front and knew she was staying in a home that the two of them often walked by when they walked the beach. He figured the home was most likely owned by some Mexican cartel leader. He asked Kekoa to identify the home's owner and find out how much money that person might have.

Kekoa laughed and said that they should diversify and get away from engaging the Mexican drug cartels. He added that he did not want the cartels bringing their feuds to Hawaii.

Brian nodded and said that he could probably pick any of the cartel leaders and they would have more than a billion dollars in banks located somewhere in the world. He added that he was curious about the one owning the beach side home, but his real interest was in US based cheating billionaires.

He smiled and added that he had no interest at mixing it up with the Mexican cartels.

He then asked if Kekoa was keeping track of Carmen and her progress in getting her US citizen ship and her personal progress on the island.

Kekoa replied that he had met with Carmen and had helped her in getting the paperwork processed to get her green card. She had enrolled in a junior college and was doing well as a waitress in the small mom and pop restaurant where Annie had helped get her hired. She had told him again to thank her sponsor for all the help and guidance that he had so far given her.

Kekoa added that she had really been impressed by Annie and had a bust drawing that Annie had made of her. She had purchased a Koa hardwood frame that she had found at the thrift store that Annie had introduced her to, and the picture was the central focus of her apartment.

Brian asked where she had finally found a place to live. He then said that they should make sure that she remained safe and was not harassed by Maite or her bodyguards.

Kekoa said that he personally knew the owners of the restaurant where she worked and that he would ask them to keep an eye out for who came in and interacted with her. He added that he had a friend that lived in the same apartment building where Carmen lived, and he would ask him to keep an eye out as well. He laughed and commented that Maite was on his home ground, and he had many friends on Maui.

Brian smiled and asked if Kekoa thought that he had more contacts than he.

That got a laugh from Kekoa, and he commented that he often forgot that Brian was a green-eyed Maui original raised by parents that were linked to Maui's royal family. He added that was more prestigious than his upbringing on the big island.

Brian asked if Kekoa was up to a walk by the beachside home where Maite was staying. He would drop Kekoa off on the beach past the home then drive by the front of the house while Kekoa scoped out the beach in front of the home. Afterwards, he would pick up Kekoa at the other end of the beach and they could go for lunch at the diner where Carmen was working and advise her to keep a low profile and stay off the beach near the house.

Once they arrived at the restaurant, Brian called Leilani and advised her of Maite's presence, her status as the person that he was working on getting in front of a judge and the relationship between Carmen and Maite. He went on to share the incident in which he had been involved in Mexico at Maite's Yucatan seaside home.

Leilani commented that he had an angry person that might be after him.

He said that she would keep an eye on Maite and if anything came up her team would be ready to act. She asked about the house where she was staying.

Once she learned about the ownership, she added that Brian should thank Kekoa for identifying the fact that the homeowner was linked with the Mexican drug cartels. This was new information for herself and the police. Knowing that information would improve the island's security.

Carmen was concerned when she learned of Matie's presence. She said that she had never met her but had heard that she was an enforcer who always got her way but who managed to stay on the good side of the drug cartels and provided a reliable human smuggling service to multiple cartels. She wanted to know what she should do.

Brian told her to stay off the beach that ran in front of the house where Matie was staying and to play on the other side of the island.

Carmen replied that given her current schedule that would be easy since she had no time lately to walk any beach.

After lunch both he and Kekoa went to the gun range. Since his return he had scheduled several extra sessions on the gun range. He knew that his ability to take out the guard at the beach had been because he had practiced and continually tried to improve. Since his return he had risen two levels and was just one level away from being at the top.

Kekoa commented on Brian's intense focus on his shooting skill and that he was being left in the dust.

Brian nodded and replied that getting hit in the middle of his chest had created an intense desire to be the best when it came to exchanging gunfire. He said nothing about the coaching he was receiving from Alex Evercrest on how to shoot out the targets bullseye while blindfolded.

The next morning, he asked Kekoa whether he could track Maite's phone location. Kekoa replied that he had picked up her phone signal the day before and had it locked into his tracking software.

She had spent the day before in her house and had taken a walk on the beach.

Maite had called several people on the island trying to locate a Brian O'Neill. She was also trying to locate Carmen Torres. Had she known that having her phone active allowed Kekoa to lock in her location she would not have been online. She successfully got the address for both people she was looking for. She was impressed with the address of the home where Brian lived. The apartment where Carmen lived was in a respectable neighborhood on the other side of the island. She really had no interest in Carmen other than she did not want her to share too much about the smuggling operation. She figured that whatever Carmen knew was already out of the bag. Her real concern was what this Brian intended to do with what he had learned.

She went online to see if she could learn anything on social media but did not find him mentioned anywhere. She decided that a direct approach might be more effective.

Brian and Kekoa were sitting on the veranda when Kekoa said that Maite was driving toward the house.

Brian looked at his watch and suggested they drive to lunch and see what would happen.

The two walked to the car and backed out to the end of the driveway. When Kekoa signaled, Brian backed out and slowly drove away. They had agreed to take lunch at their favorite luncheon location that provided open outdoor seating. Brian drove the speed limit there and Kekoa verified that Maite was following.

When they arrived at the restaurant, after verifying that Maite was parking a few rows from them, Kekoa closed his computer and put it under the seat. The two walked in and took a table at the far end of the outdoor seating area that allowed them the view of the rest of the restaurant.

It was early and most of the tables were empty. Maite was immediately identifiable when she walked in with her two bodyguards and sat a few tables from where Brian was sitting.

There were three additional pairs of men sitting at three different tables. It was clear to Brian that Maite was trying to figure out which pair she had followed. He decided to just watch to see what the approach would be for her to identify who he was.

Her two bodyguards stood up and walked up to each table and asked the names of the men sitting at each table. After the third table they returned to the table where Maite was sitting.

After a moment, Maite stood up and she walked toward he and Kekoa. She was bracketed by her two bodyguards.

Both Brian and Kekoa had their guns in their shoulder holsters. Brian simply said that they should be ready.

Maite asked if she could sit down and before he could answer she sat. Her two bodyguards sat down and exposed their guns.

Brian smiled and welcomed them and said that if they reached for their guns they would be sitting dead in their chairs before they could get a shot off. He then welcomed Maite and asked which of the two that he had shot at their previous meeting.

Maite frowned and said that he had killed one of her favorite guards and she had tracked him down to warn him that he would be the one that would die the next time gunfire was exchanged.

Brian said he was sorry to hear about the fact that her favorite bodyguard was dead, but he had fired first without warning, and he had reflexively returned the fire. He then commented that she had come a long way to just give him a warning.

He then complemented her in being able to find such a nice waterfront house to rent while she was on the island. He added that she would have to thank Andres Castillo for loaning it to her during her stay.

This seemed to catch her by surprise. She looked across the table and asked who he was and why he was looking into what she was doing or where she was living.

Brian shook his head and said that he had interest in her only because she had helped get a young lady illegally across the border and he wanted to know more about such an operation.

She asked if he was a DEA agent.

He said that he was not, but he did have contact with them.

The lunch order came and after it was delivered Brian asked if there was anything else that Maite wanted to know.

She shook her head and said that she was planning to leave the island and hoped that he would cease his activities into her operation. If he continued, then something bad might happen.

Brian shook his head and replied that threats would only increase his interest in her. He complemented her on her ability to maneuver around the various cartels in such a smooth manner and said that he understood that she had great talent. He also recognized that she had made a huge amount of money on the backs of poor Mexicans and Latin Americans and that how she had done that was his interest.

Maite stood up and said that she would take her lunch elsewhere. She led the way out of the restaurant.

Brian's radar was up, and he kept an eye in the open area where some low bushes provided some cover for anyone walking by outside. He kept a close eye as he saw the three walk by.

He and Kekoa finished lunch and were walking out to the car when Kekoa pushed him off the sidewalk.

Brian immediately spotted the bodyguard leaning on the top of the car with his gun pointed at him. He drew his gun, took a step to his right, and fired at the bodyguard's forehead. The bullet meant for him missed him, but his bullet found what he had aimed for.

After a moment, the car lurched away and sped out of the parking lot. He ran over to where the car had been parked. He found the gun, but the shooter must have been pulled into the car.

He put in a call to Leilani and let her know what had happened. A few moments later a police car pulled into the parking area and the officer walked over to where Brian was standing over the gun.

Then a host of police cars arrived, and the parking lot became a crime scene. Brian walked over to where he had been when the first shot from the bodyguard had been fired and a search for the bullet was started.

About an hour later Leilani called to let him know that Maite had been able to leave the island on a private jet to an unknow destination.

The house where she had been staying was now a crime scene as well and it was clear that Maite had not returned to it, and all her things and the bodyguard's things had been left behind.

It was not much after that that Leilani called again to let him know that the rental car had been located and there was a dead body with a bullet hole in the center of his forehead in the back seat. She complemented Brian on his shooting skill.

He said that he had learned that skill from one of the best and that on his next practice session he was going to try to shoot out the center of the target while he was blindfolded.

Leilani said that her whole team would want to be there and if he pulled it off, she would treat him to lunch.

62

Chapter 6: Getaway

Maite sat in the back seat with her dead bodyguard still bleeding from a bullet hole in his forehead. She was in a state of shock. She had expected to watch the obnoxious person, Brian, who she had met at lunch, die on his way out of the restaurant. Instead, she had pulled Pedro with a bullet hole between his eyes back into the car and then they raced for the airport to get off the island. Ray had silently driven to the airport as she called ahead and arranged for her private plane to prepare for an immediate take-off. When they got there Pedro was left unceremoniously in the back seat. She said a short prayer for him and then immediately boarded the plane. It was hard for her to keep from shaking.

The takeoff was smooth, and she then sat back to reflect on what had just happened. The attempt to kill this Brian had taken an unexpected turn. She was headed back to the mainland but had to abandon her suitcase full of clothes and personal items. She felt lucky to have made it off the island.

She was now sure that this Brian O'Neill was either very lucky or was exceptional with his weapon. She had watched his superb, smooth, and calm reaction. He had only fired his weapon once and her second bodyguard was dead.

She contemplated her situation. She felt that she had made a mistake and had underestimated her opponent. She also felt that she just did not know enough about him. He seemed to know everything about her. She on the other hand, now had the impression that he quietly and confidently wielded significant influence and power. She looked out to the endless dark blue of the Pacific and the scene from the shark movie where the captain saw the size of the shark and muttered that he was going to need a bigger boat. She decided that she needed more than two bodyguards, and she was going to need a new place other than the Yucatan. She needed a place that was isolated, easy to defend and where no one knew who she was or where she was. She had the financial means, and she was going to use it.

She dozed off and did not wake up until the bump as the plane landed in Corpus Christy. She felt lucky that she had her passport with her in her purse. The airport's custom agent came on board and cleared both she and her bodyguard. The pilot had arranged for a limo that came to the plane and picked them up. She was operating in automatic and kept going over what had just happened.

Upon arrival to her beachside Condo, she asked Ray to set up a series of bodyguard interviews. She told him she wanted to get them on board immediately and that he should pick people that he knew and who he could trust.

During her shower she thought about all the places in the Caribbean that might make a suitable getaway spot. She wanted a spot where there were few tourists and isolated from the rest of the islands.

She called up a map and randomly selected the small island of St Barthélemy and then called her realtor and asked her to check to see if there was an ocean front home available. She decided that if she were going to hide, she would do it in comfort and style. So far, she had been able to find ocean front homes and planned to find another one so she could enjoy her time on the beach. She kept thinking about the fact that her Yucatan home had been so easily found by Brian and wondered how that could have happened. She decided to use one of her alternate passports with a fake name when she made her next home purchase. She hoped that would throw off anyone looking for her.

She spent the afternoon interviewing and hiring three more bodyguards. She figured that she could buy a large enough house that had space for the herself and the four of them.

She complemented Ray in finding three additional qualified guards in such a short time.

After several hours as the Maui police worked the crime scene, Brian finally was able to leave the parking lot where the shooting had taken place. He and Kekoa returned to the house and set themselves up in the veranda.

During the wait in the parking lot Kekoa had kicked in all the computer programs that Johnnie had bequeathed to him. He had been able to track Maite's phone back to the US via a series of satellites into which he had tapped. Now on the veranda, he periodically updated Brian on Maite's location.

Brian commented that both needed to get a good night's sleep and suggested that perhaps Kekoa should plan to go home and continue the monitoring from there.

Kekoa agreed and said that he would set things up so he could get some sleep but keep track of where Maite might go.

Maite was dozing on one of her poolside reclining chairs when the realtor from St Barthélemy called and said that she could take her on a virtual tour through two beach front homes that were on sizeable pieces of land and had pools.

After touring both homes, she picked the three story one that had six bedrooms, a putting green, pool, and a great view out to the ocean. The first home was a single-story home that she had liked as well and had attracted her because it had a beautiful view, but it only had four bedrooms.

She moved on purchasing the second house.

The second house seemed appropriately priced, so she accepted the price and closed the deal. She called her lawyer and had him follow up with the realtor on St. Barthélemy.

Unknown to her, Kekoa's spy set up captured every word and every picture of the tour. He also was able to capture her instructions to her lawyer. He shared everything that he had learned with Brian.

Brian smiled and said that they should call the local realtor and close on the house that Maite had rejected. So, about the time Maite closed on her new hideaway, Brian closed on the house that she had rejected. He commented that if it were on Maui, he would have one of the most beautiful houses on the island. He added that he was going to open it up as an affordable not for profit vacation rental for the common worker.

Kekoa raised his hand and said that he was a common worker.

Brian laughed and said that he would be glad to reduce his pay so he could qualify for the status of a common worker, one that made about fifteen dollars an hour.

Kekoa laughed and said that he was happy with his current salary.

Brian then added that both would soon be able to enjoy a few days in the new home when they went to round Maite up. He suggested that Kekoa find an interior decorator to get the house prepared for their visit. He suggested that he use someone that would outfit the house in the style like their current homes on Maui.

He then reminded Kekoa that Annie and the girls were coming in that evening and that the following morning he was going to see if he could replicate Alex's blinded folded shooting out of the target center. He commented that he was nervous, but he had tried it several times and seemed to have the hang of it.

Kekoa chuckled and said that it seemed that the entire Maui police force and half of the locals were going to pack into the gun range to watch. It had become the feature event that the Range Master had advertised for the target range.

Brian said that he knew that his parents and their friends were all planning to be present and that Leilani and her team would be there. He was not sure who else, but he was sure there would be more.

Both he and Kekoa went to the airport to pick up Annie and the girls. They were both surprised at how tall both girls had grown. They were both as tall as Annie and they agreed that they were as beautiful looking as her.

Kekoa had bought Leis for the three and got a kiss and a thanks from each. After the drive back across the island he dropped them off and said he would see them in the morning.

Brian enjoyed a short evening listening to the three explain that they had arranged to see the school of their choice and that they planned to enroll for the coming year. He was pleased about their willingness to move to Maui. This had been one of his concerns and now he could relax and move on with getting them connected to all the fun they could have on Maui. He was sure they would soon make new friends as well.

They all said that they were eager to see if he could duplicate Alex's shooting exhibition.

Later Annie asked how confident he was that he could do it.

Brian said that the only obstacle that might affect him was the size of the crowd that was going to be there to watch.

Annie laughed and said that he should just imagine everyone in the crowd being naked and he would have no problem at reducing the stress of being watched.

He laughed and said that now he would need to keep from laughing while he demonstrated his gun handling skill.

The next morning, they all drove to the gun range where they were greeted outside by the crowd that had come to watch.

Kaia, Koni, and Marian gave him hugs and wished him good luck.

He was surprised to see Sister Ella and a friend was in the crowd as well. He walked over to her and gave her a hug and thanked her for coming.

The Range Master had kept everyone outside until Brian arrived.

They all entered, and Brian put his gun down on the table. After getting his gun checked, he picked it up, loaded it and positioned himself as Alex had told him. After getting into position and raising his gun, he had Annie tie the blindfold on. She gave him a kiss on his cheek and wished him good luck.

He took a deep breath and slowly and steadily pulled the trigger six times. He pointed his gun down as a thunderous cheer and loud hooting came from the crowd.

When the blindfold came off, he was able to see five holes around the edge of the center of the target and one-hole dead center. He put his gun on the table as the Range Master pulled the target in and took it off its hangers. He asked Brian to sign it and said that it would get framed and hung up in the lobby where everyone could see it. He commended that he would use it to get more people to come more often.

Brian signed the target. He smiled and mentally thanked Alex for the coaching. He now felt he was at the top of his shooting skills. He got a series of hugs and congratulations from most of those that had been observing.

He then reminded everyone that he was hosting a lunch out on the deck of the restaurant where they could watch the wind surfers and enjoy the day.

During the lunch, he had Kekoa set up a screen so he could show the home purchase that he had just made on the island of St Barthélemy. He invited his luncheon guests to enjoy a free vacation stay at this new place.

He said that he would arrange for a local agent to manage it and to schedule vacation stays and he would send out a message to them as soon as everything was set up.

He had not expected the cheer that went up but smiled and raised his glass of tea and said that they all deserved to learn that there were other places almost as beautiful as the island of Maui.

Maite would not have cheered if she had known about Brian's purchase. She was busy arranging to move into her hideaway. She had no clue that her hideaway was very visible from Hawaii. In fact, her home security camera system that Kekoa had hacked into provided both internal and external views of her new home and the surrounding grounds.

Kekoa had kept track of the activities at Maite's new home and watched as it had some renovation work done and then watched as an interior decorator moved furniture and pictures in. He was impressed with the transformation and mentioned this to Brian.

Brian said that Kekoa should get the name of the contractor and the interior decorator. If they decided the house, he had purchased needed renovation, they could meet with them when the two of them went to the island. He asked how the work with the interior decorator, to set up the house so that it would be ready for them to enjoy when they got there, was going.

Kekoa let him know that he had their local interior decorator working with the one in St Barthélemy. It seemed to him that the two were doing great.

A few days later, Brian went with Annie and the girls to their new school and listened as the principal described the curriculum and the success the school had in placing their students in prestigious colleges around the world. He listened as the girls asked a series of questions about remote learning and other special programs. It was clear to him that they had done their own research and were just verifying what they already knew.

The principal asked whether they were residents of the island and was surprised when Brian said that he had been born and raised on Maui and now owned a home overlooking a golf course. She asked what field of business he was in and when he replied that he was a lawyer she nodded and said that was a good field.

Brian was sure that what was really being asked was whether they would be able to afford the school. He was aware that the school tuition was close to that of many of the prestigious universities. He took out his check book and suggested that he pay for the tuition for the coming year.

The principle smiled and said that would be welcome. She added that books were a separate expense, and they would depend on the courses that Linda and Laurie enrolled in. She then gave him the upcoming year's tuition fee.

Brian wrote the check. Then he asked if the school offered tuition free entrance for qualified but poor students.

The principal shook her head and said that the school did not have the budget to set up such a program.

He suggested that she set up a meeting to study that situation and he would gather a group that would fund such a program.

She said that would really be of value to the school and said she would work with him to make it happen.

After leaving the school, Brian asked what was on the agenda for the remainder of the day.

Annie suggested they go to the beach, find a shady spot, and spend the rest of the day relaxing until it came time for dinner.

Laurie suggested they stop by one of the taco trucks and pick up some snacks and drinks to take out to the beach.

He nodded and said that lazing on the beach, in the shade and snacking on a fish taco was very attractive to him if everyone carried their own stuff.

74

Chapter 7: Inspired

Carmen could not believe the cycle of her luck. Her trip across the border in the false bottom of the cleaning van had ended in her arrest when she was pushed out of the van for getting mad about the condition of her clothes. She had gotten into the bottom of the cleaning van and felt herself slide along its floor. She felt something on her hands and wiped it off on her jeans. When she got across the border and got out of the van, she realized it was grease that had leaked from the rear transmission. When she complained she was pushed out of the van and left in the street. It was only a few moments later when she was stopped by the border patrol. It all happened so fast that it disoriented her. She had spent her small fortune paying for getting smuggled into the US, now she figured that her future was over.

She was sitting in the holding cell contemplating what was going to happen to her. She had been told she would be going before a judge who would decide whether she could stay or be sent back to Mexico. She had also been told that the outcome was that she most probably would be taken across the border and let go.

A deputy came to her cell and asked her if she was willing to be interviewed by a Brian O'Neill who was interested in how she had been smuggled into the country.

She has already been interviewed by two border security officers and was not sure she had anything more to share but she was curious as to why this person was interested in her case.

She followed the deputy, though she had no clue what was expected of her. After a brief introduction, this Brian person asked her about what she could remember about being smuggled into the country. He made it clear that he was interested in what she might have seen or remembered about the smuggling process and anyone that she interacted with. He had read what she had so far shared during her interrogation, and he was looking for something that she might not have thought important.

She thought for a moment and said that the only thing that she had not already told the people who had interviewed her was that the two women that were managing the smuggling operation wore uniforms with a patch on the left shoulder with the words, Maite's Cleaning Service. The other thing she remembered was that the two were not very friendly to her or the other people who they had smuggled into the country.

She smiled as Brian said, "pay dirt." He asked for a moment and made a call and asked for the person on the other end to find out about Maite's Cleaning Service.

After hanging up, he thanked her for the information and then asked if she was interested in being sponsored into the country.

It took her a minute to process what he had asked her. She verified that he was offering to sponsor her. She asked why he would do such a thing.

His response, that he could and had decided to do it, had surprised her.

He went with her to the court room and let the judge know that he would be her sponsor. Not only did he sponsor her but afterwards he took her shopping for some clean clothes and personal items, and he paid for her flight to Hawaii. That time from coming across the border to getting sponsored that she had experienced was a cycle from a very low point to an unbelievable high one.

She was Jonah who was saved from drowning when he was swallowed by a whale and then later spit out on dry land. She had been swallowed by her whale of emotions and was now being spit out into the land of paradise.

She called her parents to let them know what was happening. Their only worry was about Brian's intentions. She told them not to worry because it was clear to her that he had his mind not on her but set on the person who ran the smuggling ring that had transported her into the US.

Since her arrival to Maui, she first resided for a week in a top beach front hotel on Wailea. She had walked the beach for miles in each direction. She had eaten in several of the hotel's restaurants and enjoyed very delicious meals. She had enjoyed drinks and dancing with a variety of young men.

It was a complete change of experience, and the cost was covered by her new benefactor.

Annie Scotts, Brian's significant other, had worked with her to help her get a job, relocate to a nice apartment and to begin the process of becoming a US citizen. It became clear to her that Annie was a person to admire. She and Annie had hit it off and the two had gone shopping for some basic clothing. She was surprised when Annie did what Brian had done in the US and took her to a secondhand store where both bought a variety of clothes. The bill for both was less than a hundred dollars and she had ended up with two pant suites. She was impressed that Annie, who could afford to shop at the best stores on the island, was willing to go to a humble clothes outlet to shop.

What really impressed her even more was when during lunch, Annie took out a large drawing pad and pencil and made a sketch of her. Annie signed the picture and handed it to her.

She thought it was a super drawing of her. She gave Annie a hug and thanked her for such a nice gesture.

She recalled seeing some picture frames at the secondhand store and went back to buy a frame for her sketch.

She took a picture of the sketch and sent it back to her parents with a note of how well she had been treated up to that point and that they did not have to worry about her wellbeing.

Her mother replied with a smiley face and a heart emoji.

She was a waitress at a small restaurant for a great couple and making a reasonable amount of money.

After a few weeks she enrolled in a junior college with the intention of getting a degree. She was not sure what field she would pursue but figured that it would come to her.

Her life seemed to be on a continuous rise.

Then Brian came into the restaurant where she worked and shared the fact that Maite Flores, the leader of the smuggling gang and the person who she had helped to identify, was on the Island.

This really alarmed her. She did not know what that meant for her.

He told her to stay off the beach at Wailea but otherwise to go about her normal daily routine.

Since she had little time to go to the beach his suggestion was easy to adhere to, besides, she was on the north side of the island and when she did go to the beach it was to go para sailing and that was also on the north side.

A few weeks later she took off from work so she could watch Brian's shooting demonstration and to go to lunch afterwards. She was super impressed when blindfolded, he put five bullet holes around the bullseye and one through the center. She wondered if she could ever reach the same level of skill in whatever field she finally chose to follow. It seemed such a feat would be impossible.

She had learned that he was a lawyer who had successfully put a cheating billionaire behind bars. She knew that he was now pursuing Maite who was a very successful smuggler. She wondered if Maite qualified as a billionaire. She figured that Maite might be more dangerous than the billionaires that he had so far chased and was concerned about his safety. She would not have been so worried had she known of Brian's two gunfights with Maite's bodyguards.

She wondered if she might be able to get a job working for him. She had learned that Kekoa was Brian's computer analyst and rumor had it he was one of the world's best computer hacks. She had been looking for a more challenging job than waiting on tables. She looked at the curriculum offered at her junior college and the accounting courses caught her eye. She then wondered if Brian had an accountant on his pay role. She decided that she would get into accounting, learn the basics, and then approach Brian about becoming his accountant.

Three months later she finished her first accounting courses and felt she was ready to see about getting a job with him. She called and asked if he had time to talk with her about an idea that she wanted to share. She figured that she was not qualified to handle his millions, but she could do the basic bookkeeping and work with any financial manager that he might use.

Her mode of transportation was her bicycle. She was saving her money to buy a car, but that effort was going very slow. Her current hourly wage was six seventy-five an hour plus tips. Since she was the only waitress, the tips made a huge difference. It allowed her to meet the rent and have enough money to buy groceries. She saved the remainder to pay her school tuition and to buy her textbooks. There were only a few dollars each week left over to put into savings but if she splurged and went wind surfing there was no extra money.

The ride across the island to Brian's house took a couple of hours. She took a sandwich with her knowing that she would want something after meeting with him. It was late Saturday morning when she arrived. She was greeted at the door by Linda, one of Annie's daughters and led through the house to the veranda that faced the ocean. She could not get over how comfortable and gorgeous the home felt and looked. The entrance area had a painting of Molokini that had Annie's signatures on the lower right corner.

The six-foot-wide hallway was lined with portraits of Annie, and Brian standing on either side of Linda and Lorie. Then each person was painted sitting to the side of that painting and they were pointing to the picture. It really solidified her observation of how close the four of them seemed. She felt that she was entering a house where a loving family live.

The living room blew her mind. Over the fireplace mantle was a large painting that looked out at Molokini through the lens of two black volcano lava walls. It was stunning and made her stop as she took it in.

Linda commented that the painting was one of her mother's more stunning ones and was the one that Brian had bought despite it having the outrageous price of three hundred thousand dollars. It was the painting that had sealed his romance with her mother. She added that her mother would have given it to him just to keep him.

Carmen knew then that she was in a dream house, which held stories that she wanted to learn about.

She knew that she had to convince Brian to hire her.

Brian looked at the time. He knew that Carmen could not afford a car and asked how she had come across the island. When he learned that she had ridden her bike, he knew that Carmen had something important that she was planning to share.

He asked her to sit down and poured her a glass of iced tea.

Kekoa was sitting at a table next to where Brian was sitting and greet her with, "Aloha 'oe pehea 'oe i kēia lā nani." Carmen did not understand it completely, but she had learned enough to know that he was saying hello and most likely asking how things were going.

She smiled and was proud to answer him in Hawaiian, "Ke hana maika'i nei au" (I am doing well).

She would have to tell her two current employers that their language coaching had paid off.

Kekoa smiled, looked at Brian and said that if she had come to ask for a job, he should hire her.

Brian laughed and told Carmen she was hired and that her salary would come out of Kekoa's salary that was too high.

Carmen was a little taken aback by the back and forth and was not sure how to proceed.

Kekoa then told her not to be shy and just blurt out why she had ridden across the island to talk with Brian.

Carmen decided to take Kekoa's advice. She asked whether Brian would hire her to be his accountant?

Brian asked her if she was qualified to handle such a role.

Carmen shook her head and said that she had just finished the first portion of an accounting degree and would be able to handle the basics but would have access to the resources to cover the more complicated financial situations. She added that she would continue to improve her skills and would eventually be capable of being his financial manager. She looked at him and said that she would continue to develop herself to the point that she could shoot the center out of her financial bull's eye with her blindfold on.

Brian looked over to Kekoa and asked him what he thought.

Kekoa replied, e hoʻolimalima iā ia ma mua o kona hele ʻana i kahi ʻē aʻe." (hire her before she goes somewhere else)

Carmen only understood, "hire her." She looked expectantly at Brian.

Brian looked at her and said, "ua hoolimalimaia oe." (You're hired)

This time she understood completely, and she jumped up and gave Brian a hug and said, "Mahalo."

Brian looked at the time and said that the two of them should set up the basic working arrangements and decide on what the pay would be. He commented that he had no idea what an accountant's salary should be.

He looked at Kekoa and asked him to suggest a salary for a beginning accountant that had great understanding of the Hawaiian language.

Kekoa understood what was being asked. He would propose a salary at about eighty percent of the top wage. When he had the figure, he knew that it would blow Carmen's mind. He looked at Brian and suggested they have lunch first and then finish the discussion about the salary. He suggested their favorite place for lunch, that the whole family go so they could all welcome their new accountant.

At lunch Kekoa asked if a rare beef filet or a beef short rib appealed to anyone.

Annie commented that each person should order a different menu item and then they would all share.

Carmen said that she would take the filet and then listened as everyone selected a different item. The way that the waiter handled the order, asked if they were doing the same with the appetizer order and then brought out the table wear made it clear that everyone but her had been at the restaurant often.

He then asked about drinks, and everyone asked for water.

Brian asked for a pitcher of iced tea.

He then looked over at Kekoa and asked if he had any idea what a young, upcoming financial manger should be paid.

Kekoa shook his head and said that it was more than anyone with a good conscious should make, and he was afraid to share the figure.

Carmen was hoping for at least double her current salary.

Then Kekoa shared the figure of one hundred forty-five thousand dollars.

Carmen was so shocked that she began to cry. Her upward journey had just skyrocketed, and she was up in a cloud of stars. It took her a few moments to recover.

Brian knew that it was well beyond what she had been expecting. He waited a moment. Then with a broad smile said that if the salary were too low, he would ask Kekoa to reconsider his recommendation.

Carmen dried the tears from her eyes and replied that it was hard for her to think about such a salary. She added that she had not dreamt of such a high salary. It would change the trajectory of her life and it was hard for her to take in all the possibilities before her. She said she could not wait to share the good news with her parents.

Annie smiled and said that Brian had a knack of changing the trajectories of people's lives. Those he had a positive view of got to experience a positive trajectory. Those whom he had a negative view of had a very negative trajectory. She then complimented Carmen for sitting at the positive trajectory table.

Brian then said that he was going to give her an advance on her pay and wrote her a check for ten thousand dollars and suggested she buy herself a car so that she could get to work more easily. He added that much of her work would be able to be done from home but there would be several accounts and transactions that would need to be done at his office out on the veranda.

For the rest of the day, she was in a state of shock. She could not remember her bike ride back to her apartment. The next day at work she shared her good fortune with her bosses who congratulated her in getting a great job with such a good boss. They shared the fact that he was one of their favorite customers and always left a very good tip.

After work she rode her bike to a used car lot to see what kind of a car she could buy. She wanted to pay cash so that she would not have a monthly bill. She visited several car lots and was about to give up when she got a call from, Malia who she had met at Brian's blind folded shooting display. Malia said that she had heard that she was in the market for a used car and that she had a very reliable one that had just received its annual upkeep. She then asked if Carmen would like to see and drive it.

Carmen knew then that she was living in and benefiting from the tight community that kept an eye on each other. Malia agreed to meet her at the University Student Union. The two of them walked out to a polished black sedan that sported shiny tires. There were no scratches on the paint and the interior leather seats looked like new. Malia handed her the keys and suggested that she drive it to see if it met her expectations. Before she left the parking lot Carmen knew she wanted to have the car. She asked about the price. Malia smiled and said that she was hoping to get three thousand for it. Carmen immediately said that she would buy it.

Malia took the title out of the glove compartment and signed the back and said they should stop by the bank and get everything processed. She asked if Carmen would take her to the Honda dealer to pick up her new car.

Carmen called her parents to share the good news and the fact that she was sure she could find some people on the island to sponsor them into the US.

88

Chapter 8: Closing In

Brian and Kekoa monitored Maite's movement daily. She very quickly left the US for her new home on St Barthélemy. Kekoa was able to hack into her home security system and they were able to watch the activities taking place in the house and on the surrounding property grounds. The grounds had an impressive layout that featured a putting green on one side of the house, a large pool with a Jacuzzi situated on one end that provided a view out toward the bay waters. A long red brick walkway, leading to the beach, split the lush well-trimmed grass of the yard into two equal halves that had matching flower beds and rose bush hedges. The two of them agreed that the grounds and scenery were impressive.

They decided that Maite had an easygoing daily routine of an early morning walk along the beach, then breakfast on her veranda and finally she would spend time putting on the golf green before going to the beach to relax. During her beach time, she would spend time on the phone with the various people running her factories and managing her smuggling ring.

It was clear that she had trusted, and capable people positioned in her leadership positions. It was a demonstration of her top management skills that impressed both. They decided she would have made a good leader of any major company.

This ability to eavesdrop in on her conversations allowed Kekoa to find out that both he and Brian were being watched by some person on Maui. Soon after, Kekoa learned that a sniper had been hired to kill Brian.

This surprised both and it changed the nature of their pursuit of her.

The focus then turned to finding out who this sniper was.

Kekoa could not determine who the sniper was by name but by tapping into the Maui based observer's phone and he learned when the sniper would be arriving to the island. He was able to get a clear facial shot from the airport security camera that focused on the arrivals coming down the escalator. He ran the picture through the police databases that he had access to expecting to get a hit but instead came up empty handed.

He sent the picture to Johnnie and asked him to see if he could identify the person. A short time later Johnnie replied that he had found a young version of the person. He added that since an arrest made more than twenty-five years before, there was nothing more in the databases about him. He was invisible in all the databases that he had access to.

Kekoa shared what he had learned with Brian.

Brian said that it was time to engage Leilani. He said that he needed her help to eliminate the threat of being assassinated.

Kekoa followed the observer's car as it left the airport by tracking the location of the observer's phone. He found out that the sniper had checked into the hotel, on the beachfront, directly down from Brian's house. This person had registered as James Skaters and had rented the penthouse suite that was on the top floor. It didn't take Kekoa long to get into the security cameras on that floor. He was then able to observe the luggage for James Skaters being delivered. There was now a golf club bag included in the luggage. Kekoa checked back to see what had been picked up at the airport. The golf bag had not been part of the luggage that had been picked up.

He and Brian speculated that the golf bag carried the sniper rifle.

Kekoa had connected into the security camera in the hallway, and the security cameras that were mounted on the roof of the hotel. He and Brian reviewed what could be seen. The security cameras on the roof could be aimed at Brians home and produce a clear image. One of the cameras could also see most of the roof top.

Brian in turn let Leilani know what was going on.

Leilani went to the hotel and arranged access the roof area. She went up and assessed the layout and decided that the roof ventilator fans, and other roof top equipment provided the cover that she and her team would need.

She walked over to where she thought the best spot to get a clear shot to Brian's pool and Veranda area. She called and asked Kekoa to access the roof cameras and take a picture of her as she stood at the spot where she felt the shooter would be.

Both Kekoa and Brian agreed that she was in the right spot.

When she was back to the car, she assigned Malia, and James, to tail James if he left the hotel.

Early the next morning James, carrying a putting golf club, took a walk across the golf course and then left a bottle standing at the edge of the bushes at the border of Brian's property. He then walked back to the beach and returned to the hotel from the beach side.

A few moments later, Kekoa watched as James came out on the roof carrying his golf bag. He extracted a rifle with a huge scope and a silencer that made the rifle look like a cannon. Kekoa trained one camera on James and another on the bottle at the edge of the bushes. James loaded one shell into the sniper rifle and then took aim of the bottle. Kekoa saw that the bullet had hit just below where the bottle was standing. James ejected the first bullet, put the empty casing back into a holder and then put a second bullet into the rifle.

The next shot hit and smashed the metal bottle. It flew into the air and landed in the sand pit below.

James put everything away and left the roof with his golf bag.

A short time later, Malia and David followed James as he again walked back across the golf course, dug out the bullet that had missed, and picked up what was left of the bottle and put his finger on the spot on the bottle where the bullet had impacted. He picked up what was left of the second bullet. He put everything in a brown paper bag and walked down to the beach. He discarded the bag with the bottle in a trash container.

David retrieved the bag and put it in an evidence bag.

Brian, Leilani, Kekoa. Malia and David discussed what they had learned. Brian conjectured that James would next be determining when he should pull off the assassination. He said that each morning he would stand out at the edge of the veranda as if looking out on the waters beyond the hotel.

That position would provide a clear shot for James.

Leilani commented that seemed dangerous.

Brian agreed but added that she needed to catch James in the act of getting ready to shoot. He added that he was counting on her team to keep James from shooting.

Leilani said that her team would be on the roof ready to catch him in the act.

The next day Brian stood out on the veranda. Kekoa caught James standing on the hotel roof with a pair of binoculars. The same happened on the second day.

Each day, Leilani, Malia, and David were in position to intervene.

On the third day, James came out on the roof with his golf bag.

Kekoa verified that Leilani and her team were in place.

Brian had his complete Kevlar body suit on. He had on a straw hat to hide the fact that he was even wearing his Kevlar head gear. He had decided to take every precaution he could. He hoped that Leilani and her team would be fast enough to keep him from getting shot.

Leilani and her team were standing behind some air vents and air conditioning units ready to make their move.

James went into action much faster than Leilani and her team were anticipating. He had his sniper rifle loaded, was able to pull it out and fire even as Lelani rushed out to stop him.

She rushed out and yelled that it was the police, and he was under arrest, but he had already taken the shot.

He stood up, pulled a pistol from his shoulder holster, and took a shot at Leilani and hit her but she shot him three times and then he was then hit six additional times as Malia and David took their three shots. He died instantly.

Leilani had fired her gun but then fell to her knees where she would have collapsed but Malia embraced her and held her up.

Leilani realized that her Kevlar vest had saved her, but she was still shocked at being hit. She wondered how Alex continued to function so effectively after having experienced similar situations multiple times.

On the veranda, a surprised Brian stumbled backwards as the bullet hit him in the chest. He laughed a little hysterically and shouted out that Leilani had been too slow.

Kekoa rushed over and helped Brian stand up. They then both put their fingers through the hole in his shirt that was almost dead center on his chest. Kekoa commented that for that distance it was an excellent good shot.

Brian laughingly agreed. He shook his head and asked if Leilani and her team had captured James.

Kekoa went back to his monitor and replied that they had put about nine holes into a now dead sniper.

Annie came out on the veranda and took in the scene. She was surprised and a little angry. She now understood Brian's request that she not come out to her normal pool side painting area. She went over to him and put her finger in the hole of his shirt and asked if he had planned this drama.

Brian shook his head and replied that the shooter had been faster than Leilani's team, but the shooter had paid the ultimate price.

Annie smiled and said that he was getting to be as bad as Alex, and she hoped that his cases would not all be this active.

Brian sat down and took a sip of his iced tea, closed his eyes, and replied that he had Alex to thank for having insisted on the Kevlar outfit. It had now saved him twice.

He asked Kekoa to drive him over to the Hotel so they could go up and join Leilani and her team.

When they got up to the roof area, a police officer stopped them and said that they could not enter the crime scene. Kekoa pulled out his badge, pointed to Brian and said, "He's with me."

The officer looked at the badge and lifted the crime scene yellow tape.

Brian laughed and asked how long Kekoa had been moonlighting and if he was dissatisfied with his current salary.

Kekoa shook his head and said that Leilani had insisted on deputizing him the last time they had discussed the situation. She said that it might be useful in the future.

Leilani was sitting back on one of the vent units being attended by an EMT.

Brian walked over and said he had come over so that he could be attended to as well. He put his finger through the hole in his shirt.

Leilani responded by putting a finger through the hole in her blouse. She commented that James had a very fast draw.

Malia pointed to where the coroner was examining the body and added that he had a fast draw, but they had all shot him three times and that he was three times dead.

Brian sat down next to Leilani and thanked her and her team for taking care of James. He asked about the person who had facilitated James and provided him the weaponry.

Leilani let him know that he had been arrested and charged as an accessory to attempted murder.

The EMT came over and checked him out and commented that he was going to have a much bigger bruise than Leilani. He asked the caliber of bullet that had hit him.

Leilani pointed at the weapon that was still lying near James' body and commented that it was whatever caliber that cannon had fired.

He commented that both were very lucky and asked if they wanted any pain medication for later. Both declined and said they had their own at home.

Brian then commented that luck had nothing to do with it. It was the high skill level of the Maui detective unit that was on display.

The next day they all met at Leilani's office to review what had happened and what needed to happen next. Leilani held up the grey colored rifle and commented that it was one of the most accurate weapons used by snipers. It was in use in many law enforcement sniper units across the world. It was near the top of line though now there were a few new rifles that were even better. She held up the revolver and said that she had been lucky that it was a thirty-eight versus something of a higher caliber.

She commented that the thirty-eight had left a hand sized bruise in the middle of her chest that still hurt.

She looked at Brian and asked when he was going to arrest Maite and put her behind bars.

He shared that he and Kekoa were planning to arrest her within the next few days.

He then shared the fact that the two of them had purchased a home on St Barthélemy that was on the same island where Matia had moved.

He planned to invite her to move back to the US where he would arrest her and take her to court for money laundering and not paying her taxes.

Leilani chuckled and said he would have to share how he would invite Maite to go with him back to the US. She was sure that there would be an interesting twist to that journey. She asked why he was not charging her with attempting to assassinate him.

He replied that he did not want to be directly involved in the trial and was satisfied to have her sentenced for the crimes that would keep him out of the spotlight and still put her away for a very long time.

He and Kekoa had worked with the realtor to outfit the home that they had purchased on St Barthélemy. Kekoa pulled up the cameras that allowed him to give everyone a tour of the interior of the home and the view of the grounds and the ocean beyond.

The interior decorator had outfitted the home the way that the interior decorator on Maui had suggested and the place had taken on the impressive look of a home magazine layout.

Leiloni commented on the great appointment of the interior and then added the ocean scene was outstanding. She asked what Brian intended doing with a house in the Bahamas.

Brian smiled and said that he was going to invite the entire Maui detective team to spend a vacation there on his dime. He added that afterwards he was going to make it available, at a very low cost, to anyone in the middle to lower income status.

Leilani smiled and said that, based on what he paid people, her whole team would qualify as being in the middle to lower income group.

Brian laughed and said that her team certainly deserved more for saving his life and he would up the ante to three fully paid for vacations at his St. Barthélémy beach front home that could be scheduled to fit their vacation schedules.

Ron Mueller

<u>Chapter 9: Moon Curser Night</u>

When the kill verification call from her contact in Maui did not come in, Maite knew that something had gone wrong. She was very disappointed since she had paid what she thought was a premium to get the top assassin to kill this Brian worm. She hoped that at least he had been critically wounded.

She contacted her second informant on the island. He verified that the assassin had been killed and that her other informant had been arrested. He said that as far as he knew, the target of the assassination had survived with no injuries.

She instructed her remaining Maui informant to keep track of Brian and let her know his movements.

She spent the rest of day contemplating the situation and decided that in the short term she would let that issue go and concentrate on the running of her multiple businesses and in enjoying her new home. She figured that if she let things settle down, she could get back to visiting her business interests and eventually be comfortable in returning to her condominium in Texas. She desired to use her remaining good luck in growing her business.

Except for the Maui glitch, everything else seemed to be in great shape. The only nagging thing was that the Hawaiian rash that seemed to be consistently coming back to haunt her and always eluded being wiped out.

All her businesses were turning in record profits. She figured that soon she would be able to step away from the business and just enjoy herself on the beach. She worried about not having some other substantial activity to take up her time. Her travel desires would take up a couple of years, but she was looking for something more. She kept pondering about what else she might do. She slowly came to realize that she was doing what she wanted to do.

Back in Maui, Brian and Kekoa were getting ready to make the trip to St Barthélemy. After realizing that taking a series of commercial flights would extend the travel time to almost two days and along with a ton of waiting for the connections, Brian arranged to fly on a private charter. The plan included a stop in Mexico City to pick up Eduardo. After a short one-day layover in Mexico City they would go on to the island.

They left early in the morning before sunrise, when they arrived at the private airport in Mexico City, Eduardo surprised them by introducing his replacement, Jorge Cruz. He then added that he was going to cross the border into the US, and he would be the US DEA agent that would arrest Maite.

Eduardo volunteered that his good friend Harol Zimmerman had helped him get his new job. He added that he liked the San Antonio area would most likely be where he would have his office and that he would be seeking to have Maite's trial held there.

Brian welcomed Jorge and then congratulated Eduardo for getting a job with the DEA.

Later that evening, they were out having dinner at an outdoor venue in the center of the city, when suddenly a truck screeched around the corner.

Brian took one look, saw a pickup truck with a machine gun mounted behind the cab, shouted for everyone to get down and drew his gun. Both he and Kekoa simultaneously responded as the mounted fifty caliper machine gun began to fire. They shot and killed the gunner and then shot two more of the men firing from the back of the pickup. Finally, they shot out the left front tire and hit the driver with the last of their rounds.

Though it seemed like an eternity, the entire incident took less than thirty seconds.

Two people sitting in a nearby table were hit, but not critically wounded.

The local police seemed to swarm in from all fronts. Eduardo and the Jorge interacted with them. A short time later Eduardo returned and said that he had vouched for them. He had convinced the police to focus on the men in the pickup truck and on the people that had been hurt. He did ask the two of them whether their weapons were legally registered in Mexico.

Brian assured him that both he and Kekoa had Mexican permits for the weapons.

Jorge asked when Brian and Kekoa had become such accurate shots. He said that he had quickly examined the three in the back of the pickup. He said that they all had been wearing bullet proof vests and that they had each been killed by bullets to the head. He added that hitting them while the truck was moving was a daunting task.

Both commented that they practiced twice a week, but this had been their first time using their weapons in an actual gun battle. They both commented at having been able to take out the gunner on the fifty-caliber machine gun.

Eduardo took in all the activity in the open eating area and suggested that they move inside and finish their dinner there. He added that he would continue to interface with the local police until everything was settled and the area cleared.

Later during the dinner, he suggested that they leave early the next morning and continue to the island. This would ensure that they would not be delayed by the gun battle follow up investigation.

Brian wondered how the attack had been planned. He figured that Maite had more than one person on Maui that had been keeping track of them. He pointed this out to Kekoa and that she had dealt with people more dangerous than the two of them and she had the money to buy all the help she needed. He wondered how much she was willing to continue spending to get him out of her hair.

He commented that she most likely would soon learn about what had happened in Mexico City. He asked the pilot to put in plans for a flight to Puerto Rico. Once they were in the air and on their way, he asked the pilot to revise the flight plan and go directly to St Barthélemy. He hoped to keep Maite in the dark long enough to 'arrest' her and take her back to Mexico.

The private plane featured comfortable seats and had full beds for all three of them. This allowed them to do a full day's work and take a quick nap before their arrival.

The two-thousand-mile flight to the island allowed them plenty of time to plan and decide how they would arrest Maite and get her to go back to the US.

Eduardo asked which crossing from Mexico into the US Brian was planning to use to get Maite to cross over.

Brian replied that El Paso had been the border crossing that he had planned to use.

Eduardo suggested they do something like a previous experience he had in getting a person to willingly cross the border into the US. He pointed out that the crossing would only be legal if they could get Maite to sign an agreement to cross the border with Brian as her host. He smiled and said that he could incentivize her to sign the agreement by making the alternative be to spend time in a Mexican jail with the rumor she was a lesbian. He said he figured she would know the consequence of being considered a lesbian who had taken advantage of the poor.

Brian shook his head and commented that Eduardo played a hard hand.

By late afternoon, the pilot let them know that he had made landing arrangements and would soon be getting ready to land.

Eduardo asked how they were going to get around on the island.

Kekoa replied that a driver and limo would be at the airport to pick them up.

The pilot informed them that a border agent would come on board and check their passports and collect the entry fees that applied.

After landing, their passports were checked. Brian and Kekoa both had to pay a three-hundred-dollar entry fee. Eduardo had no entry fee because he was from Mexico. He commented that it was the first time that being a Mexican citizen had paid off.

The driver and his host companion took their luggage and led the way to a shiny black stretch Lincoln. The host introduced the driver as Tony and gave his name as Dillon.

The three of them got in and sat in luxurious black leather seats. A small built-in cooler was conveniently located between each of the four back seats. A table split the back into two and had menus held by fixed holders. The table was designed to be able to have its passengers eating while riding. It had cup, plate and utensil holders carved into its top. Brian commented on the luxurious interior.

Dillon pointed to the menus and said they were a suggestion and that anything they might want would be readily available. He added that he had only put in a variety of drinks into the coolers but would gladly provide anything else they might want. He pointed to a small cabinet and said that very good liquor was also available.

Brian suggested that they first go to their house and afterwards he would like to go to dinner and on the return stop at a grocery to stock up on a variety of food.

It took less than ten minutes to get to the house.

Tony and Dillon followed Brian, Kekoa and Eduardo into the house and then put the luggage in the rooms each of them were staying in.

Brian, Kekoa and Eduardo took a walk down to the beach front. The calm of the late afternoon had small waves rolling along almost parallel to the beach. Eduardo commented that the cove in front of the house seemed to face the northeast and would provide a beautiful sunrise. He looked back at the house and commented on its open design with the ceiling that clearly seemed to be more than ten foot high. He added it was one of the more beautiful homes he had been in, and it was very well appointed.

Brian commented that Maite had rejected this house and had chosen one farther south that faced directly east. He figured she had liked that home better. The key difference for him was that her house was a two story, six bedroom, and this house was a large single-story, four bed room house.

They returned to the house and asked to go to a restaurant that faced to the west where they could enjoy the sunset.

After dinner and stopping to purchase a long list of groceries, they returned to the house. After putting everything away they agreed that a good night's sleep would be what they all needed.

The next morning, Brian was at the kitchen counter that surrounded a six-burner gas stove with a large vent hood overhead. He had just started to fry his two eggs when Kekoa walked in. He asked what he might want for breakfast.

Kekoa said that a cup of coffee, two over easy eggs and a slice of buttered toast would be great.

Brian put two pieces of toast into the toaster, poured a cup of coffee, put the two eggs on a plate and put everything in front of Kekoa.

Eduardo walked in, took one look, and said he would love to get the same.

Brian cooked up two more breakfasts and then sat down.

He said that they should plan to spend the day enjoying the island. He figured that sometime the next day they should 'arrest' Maite and begin their journey back to Ciudad Juárez. He added that once they landed, he wanted to cross into the US as soon as possible.

Eduardo asked how Brian was planning to make the arrest.

Brian asked Kekoa to bring up the various cameras that they had access to at Maite's house and grounds.

They found that there were two people patrolling the grounds and two people in the house. Maite seemed to move around from the living room to the veranda that faced the ocean. It all seemed very relaxed.

Kekoa pointed out that there were no dogs so at least they could enter the grounds and not get attacked. He went to the computers connection into the security monitoring system and said that there were motion detectors that seemed to be overlapped in such a fashion that there were no clear paths to the house, but he would be able to turn off any sensors that were in the path that they would use.

Kekoa commented that the security system in the house was as elaborate as the one for the yard but once again he could turn off all of it or just the parts that they needed to be turned off.

Eduardo commented that only the human element was not directly in their control.

Brian agreed. He added that he would like to get Maite out of the house without her bodyguards knowing about it. He suggested they wait until she went up to her room for the night and make the arrest there. They could then leave with her and go directly to the airport.

Kekoa suggested they take a taxi to Maite's home. He pointed out that though they seemed to have rented an honest driver and host they had no way of knowing who the two were connected to and talking to.

Eduardo nodded and said that was good thinking. He agreed and said that they could bring Maite to the airport and once in the air they could cancel the services of the car.

Brian added one more twist to the plan by saying that they should get dropped off two houses away and walk back to Maite's property. Then they should arrange for a pickup at a home a few houses away in the opposite direction. That way they would throw off any cab drivers that might be on her payroll.

Brian then suggested that they go shopping for their next evening's adventure. He thought that a basic black outfit would look good on all of them. He walked back to his room and brought out a box, handed it to Eduardo, and told him it was a Christmas gift.

Eduardo laughed and said that it was the middle of the summer. He opened the box and took out a full Kevlar suit. He looked to Brian and said that was much more than a simple Christmas gift. He tried on the jacket and said that it was exactly the right size. He then asked if Brian was expecting to have a gun battle.

Brian replied that he was not, but he had experienced the fact that you did not plan to have a gunfight, but you should plan to make sure you survived the ones that you got inadvertently involved in.

They all went to a boutique shop and felt lucky that each of them was of a different size and each of their clothing choices was available. The black shirts turned out to be a dark grey, but the suits were a flat black that was either a herring bone or plain design. The shop owner tried to get them to buy hats and gloves, but they declined. Brian paid for the three suits, and they each carried their boxed purchases out to the limo.

Once they were back to their house, Brian commented that he hoped not to get any bullet holes in his new expensive suit.

Eduardo commented that he too would not want bullet holes in his expensive suit and asked how much he owed Brian.

Brian responded that the cost would go into the case's expenses and would be treated as business expenses.

Kekoa knew that the cost would go into Brian's personal account so that it would not show up in any follow up of the case spending reviews.

The next day was spent swimming and walking along the beach during the early part of the morning.

One of the side projects that Kekoa had been working on was to hire a housekeeper that would take care of the house while they were away. He interviewed several and chose the one he felt most comfortable with.

Brian's side project was to work with the realtor to set up a property management agreement. This turned out to be relatively easy since it gave the realtor a year-round salary that made it very attractive to the realtor.

He was able to arrange with Tony and Dillon to be the driver of anyone that the realtor set them up with and that she would handle their service charges. He felt good about getting these things settled and suggested they all pack and get ready to leave. He said that once they left, they would not be returning to the house.

Kekoa arranged for the cab to take them to a home a few addresses from their intended destination.

The three arrived just as the sunset and were able to walk in the grey of the evening up to the front of Maite's property and put their suitcases out of sight in the bushes. They then strolled undetected up to the side entrance of her house. They all entered and made their way up the stairs that went from the kitchen up the back to the upstairs hallway. They all entered Maite's bedroom and took strategic positions.

Kekoa sat down in the chair that was to the back side of the bedroom door.

Eduardo took a position in the bathroom entrance.

Brian sat down at the makeup vanity that was just past the bathroom entrance.

Then they waited.

It turned out to be a rather long wait before the door opened and Maite walked in. When she turned on the light she froze.

Kekoa gave her a slight push and closed the door.

She looked at Brian and asked how he had been able to get around all the security.

Brian smiled and said that he had a wizard that knew how to whisk them in.

He said that he had come to escort her on a trip to her condominium in Texas.

She shook her head and said she had no intention of going there with him.

Brian stood up and walked into her walk-in closet and came out with a midsized suitcase. He opened it and said that she could pack it with what she would normally take for a few days of vacation, or he would do it for her.

He walked over to her and took her phone out of her hand. He smiled and said that he did not want her to call or signal her bodyguards because he did not want to kill any of them.

Maite cursed under her breath and began to pack her suitcase. She commented that she did not think they would get off the island. She said that when that happened, she would make sure all three of them would once and for all be pushing up flowers from about six feet below.

Once she had packed, they made their way out into the hallway.

As soon as they closed her bedroom door, Maite shouted out for help.

One of her bodyguards came out into the hallway with his gun at the ready.

Brian did not hesitate but immediately put a bullet through the guard's forehead. He then pushed Maite toward the backstairs. Kekoa took the lead going down and as he cleared the steps, he fired his weapon.

A second bodyguard was dead. Neither guard had been able to fire their weapons.

Both Brian's and Kekoa's weapons had silencers so there was no sound of gunfire to draw the other guards.

They made it to the edge of the property and walked casually away and were picked up by the cab Kekoa had called.

The trip to the airport took less than ten minutes and a few minutes later they were in the air on their way to Ciudad Juárez, Mexico.

Ron Mueller

Chapter 10: Crossing Over

Maite sat silently in her seat. She was livid, furious, enraged. She could not understand how three people could pass through the security system on her property, get by her guards, and get into her bedroom. Then as they left two of her defending guards were shot and most likely killed. She was then surprised that the flight from the island was on a private charter. If it had been a normal commercial flight, she was sure she would have been able to get free just by claiming to be kidnapped. As it was, she was handcuffed to the armchair of her seat, and was helpless. Her desire was to stab and kill the person sitting across from her with a dull knife.

She hoped her emergency message that she had sent from her phone was being acted upon so that she could get free when the plane landed. Once that happened, she would personally stomp this Brian to death.

She sat facing her now most hated adversary, one she had failed three times to kill.

She wondered where they were going. She decided to ask. The answer came from the Mexican agent. She wondered why he was involved.

Eduardo explained that she would determine her ultimate destination. He then explained that she had two choices. The first was to enter willingly into the United States with Brian. The second was to be sent to a Mexican prison to await trial for smuggling.

She replied that she preferred the Mexican jail. She knew that once there she would most likely be able to bribe her way out. In the US she would most likely face a more serious situation with little hope of staying out of jail. She knew she could be standing trial for attempted murder, fleeing the scene of a crime and several other likely charges.

Eduardo explained that she might want to reconsider the choice of staying in Mexico and being held since a trans woman who took money from poor workers to enrich herself would not last long in a Mexican prison.

She laughed and said that she was all woman and not a trans woman.

Eduardo smiled and said that it did not matter that she was all woman, what mattered was what the inmates and the guards at the prison thought. He said that the rumor about her would begin the day she arrived at the prison.

She looked at Brian and commented that he did not play fair.

Brian looked at her and asked if her going to Hawaii and having one of her guards try to kill him, or if her hiring an assassin to kill him or if her having him attacked in Mexico City was playing fair.

Maite stared back at him and said she thought of him as some sort of slimy snail that needed to be stepped on and squashed. She then added that she was hoping to get out of the situation she was currently in and personally stomp on him and squash him.

Kekoa signaled to Brian and pointed to his computer. They went to the back of the plane where Kekoa highlighted an emergency message sent out from Maite's phone to someone in Mexico. It simply said 'kidnapped, take action.'

Brian wondered who that might have gone to and what action Maite might have preplanned. He asked Kekoa to see if he could determine if her phone was being tracked.

A few moments later, Kekoa nodded and said that it was.

Brian figured that the person in Mexico would check what flights were approaching from the Caribbean and then get the flight plans. That person could then track the phone, identify the flight, and keep track of the plane. It would then be easy to have some air traffic controllers have the plane taxi to a place where a simple trap could be executed. When they stopped at the designated location, they would be sitting ducks in a shooting gallery.

He looked at the time and realized that they would be landing at three in the morning and the airport would be like a ghost town.

He had Eduardo contact Jorge and have him arrange for a safe location for the plane to taxi to. He added that Jorge should ensure that the person in the tower only send the location unloading location message after the plane had landed and was taxing in.

As they were landing, he watched Maite and noticed that she seemed to relax and sit back in her seat and suppress a smile. He would have to tell her later that she would make a terrible poker player.

The plane landed and the pilot followed his instructions of where to taxi the plane.

Maite sat up in anticipation and after having the handcuffs removed was eager to deplane.

A black van came up to the plane and Jorge stepped out and signaled to Eduardo who led the way down the steps from the plane.

Maite looked around and frowned as she went down the steps and then was guided into the Van and handcuffed to her seat arm rest.

Brian enjoyed her puzzled look as he and Kekoa entered the van. He quietly said, "Checkmate" and sat down.

Eduardo was sitting next to her and asked if she was ready to sign the agreement to enter the US.

She turned and looked over her shoulder and commented that he was better at chess than she and took the pen from Eduardo and signed the document next to the x on the line at the bottom of the document. Eduardo had Jorge notarize it and then he handed the paper to Brian.

He smiled and commented that staying out of a Mexican prison and betting on getting a good lawyer in the US was the better choice.

The van driver said that a truck was making a very fast approach as if it was going to slam into the van.

Brian slipped over the back seat and prepared to open one of the back doors. When the first bullets hit the van, he opened the door, shot out the two front tires of the on-coming truck and immediately closed the door.

The van driver said that the truck had skidded of the highway and flipped down the median for about a hundred feet.

Brian climbed back, got into his seat, and said, "checkmate."

A few moments later they arrived at the border. On the Mexican side of the border, they were greeted by an IRS agent who was accompanied by a Mexican Border Security officer. The security officer looked at the consent letter that Brian handed him, nodded, and signaled that the van could cross over.

The van drove across the bridge to the border crossing office building on the US side. There they all got out and walked in Once inside, they were led into an office where they were asked to sit down.

Joe Brown, the IRS leader from Cincinnati walked in and introduced Randolf Task as the IRS agent that was to lead the prosecution of Maite for money laundering and not paying taxes on more than three billion dollars.

He then introduced a lawyer that would initially represent Maite until she either agreed to the arrangement or hired a different lawyer of her choice.

He asked Maite whether she wanted to spend a few moments to discuss her situation with her assigned lawyer before deciding to accept him as her representative.

Maite looked at Brian and asked him if she could trust the assigned lawyer.

Brian smiled and said that he had never met the lawyer, but he was sure that he was qualified and that there were no strings attached to him and he could be trusted to represent her.

Maite nodded and replied that she would accept the lawyer but would like to spend a few moments discussing the situation with him.

Joe nodded and said she could take as much time as she needed to discuss the situation with her lawyer. He suggested that the rest of them go to the cafeteria for a cup of coffee or some other refreshments and give the two of them time and privacy.

Once in the cafeteria, Randolf shared the fact that he lived in San Antonio and was working to get the case decided there. He admitted that the case would be one of the biggest cases that he and his team had so far undertaken. He explained that he had reached out to Joe because of his recent handling of a similar case in which Brian had been involved. He looked at Brian and said that his reputation for bringing in wayward billionaires was getting internal IRS press. He asked if Brian knew where all Maite's money was hidden.

Brian said that he hoped that he was getting a positive reputation. He pointed to Kekoa and said that he would provide all the information that would allow Randolf to get the needed information from four offshore banks and two banks in Texas where the money was located. He added that there were also four companies that would be holding additional funds that might be pertinent but that would be for the IRS to decide. He made the point that the IRS would need to gather all the evidence that would be used in court themselves because the information being provided was not useable in court.

Kekoa handed the agent a thumb drive and said that all the information was clearly documented in a file folder for each bank and there were separate file folders for each of the businesses, and the three homes owned by Maite. The material, if duplicated by the IRS would give them an airtight case.

Randolf looked over to Joe, held up the thumb drive and said, "just as you predicted." He looked at Brian and asked if there was anything else that he should know.

Brian smiled and said except for the three attempted murders that could also be brought against Maite if they were needed, he had nothing to get in the way of a quick trial for money laundering and failing to pay taxes on her billions of dollars. He added that he would be returning to his office to begin his quest of finding the next billionaire that merited his attention. He added that San Antonio was a beautiful city with a lot of history and he and Kekoa would be at the disposal of the IRS and would welcome visiting and being in court if necessary.

Eduardo said that he would like to share the fact that he was now an official DEA agent. He would be working in San Antonio, and would be following the case, and would also be available as needed.

Brian congratulated him on his new job and suggested that they celebrate it that evening at dinner at a place of his choosing.

They returned to the meeting room where Maite and her lawyer were waiting.

Randolf took over the meeting. He said that he had arranged for a judge to charge Maite on the following day. She would be held under arrest and would be confined in her room in a hotel not far from the US Federal Courthouse. After the arraignment she would be moved to San Antonio where she would most likely be held in prison since he considered her a flight risk.

Maite looked at Eduardo and asked if there would be any bad rumors at the prison where she would be held.

Eduardo shook his head and said that none that he would start.

She looked over to Brian and said that she was glad that he had made sure she packed her suitcase for her vacation. She added that she doubted that it would be the vacation she had been dreaming of.

Brian nodded and agreed that her future would be very different. He then suggested they all call it a day.

After Maite left with her police escort, he asked where the rest of them were staying and learned that they would be at the same hotel as Maite. He then asked where a good place would be to go for a dinner that he and Kekoa would host.

Eduardo suggested a barbeque restaurant with which he was familiar.

They all agreed that barbeque sounded good. Randolf commented that Texas barbeque was the best in the world. That elicited a comment from Joe who said that it was Cincinnati barbeque that was the better tasting one. The banter went on as they left and went to the hotel.

After getting a few hours sleep and then going to the restaurant, Randolf asked why Brian was focused on wayward billionaires.

The discussion led Brian to admit that he had always felt like the very rich seemed to get away with doing things that ordinary people would have gotten into a great deal of trouble if they did them. That had led him to examine the lives of billionaires more closely.

He found that many billionaires had inherited most of their money and they were more like spoiled children only on a grander scale.

He found that those who had made their billions by producing something of value were often super aggressive, but most were ethical and fair. They seemed to have the knack at making the right financial decisions and making moves that made them successful.

Then there were those that made their money by playing the stock market. They were smart about reading the financial, social, and governmental situations and making the right choices. In another words, they knew how to gamble legally and win more often than they lost.

He commented that each of the billionaire groups he had described bothered him because they got to pay lower taxes than most hard-working people and they enjoy a life that was ensured by the laws they had lobbied for.

The group that he was pursuing was the handful that were outright cheats and committed illegal acts. That was the group that Maite was a part of. She had unsuccessfully tried multiple times to kill him. The case against her was not for trying to kill him. If she were convicted, she would go to prison for not paying her taxes. This would take her out of action and in his estimation, she would suffer more than if he pressed for a greater punishment based on her attempts to kill him.

He was now convinced that having billionaires like her face the punishment for tax evasion and money laundering was the way to handle the situation. It provided a case that could be proven by checking tax records and figuring out where the money was hidden and the time limits for the crimes did not apply.

Randolf nodded and said that if Brian continued at the pace he had set, the reward money for this case might take him a long way to joining the billionaire camp.

Brian nodded and said that becoming a billionaire was not a goal for him. He had already set up one organization to provide funds for young teens who had not been adopted and needed guidance in transitioning into normal society when they reached eighteen. He had also made several large donations to two organizations focused on aiding young adults that had experienced traumatic incidents and needed psychiatric counseling and support getting back to being productive individuals.

Randolf nodded and commented that Joe had let him know that the reward he had coming from the Cincinnati case was to be awarded the coming week. He smiled and added that the wheels of Justice were slow, and the IRS reward wheel was slower.

The next day at court, Maite entered wearing a black pant suit and sat down at the defense table. She looked over at Brian and quietly commented that the orange for the day was black.

The judge entered and asked the defense what the defendant's plea to the charges of money laundering and not paying her taxes of more than three billion dollars were.

The not guilty plea was entered into record.

Maite was surprised that her attempts to kill Brian had not been part of the charges. She thought for a moment, looked over at Brian, and gave him a thumbs up. She knew then that he was not vindictive but focused on being very successful.

The judge then declared that Maite had been judged a flight risk and would be held in the San Antonio federal detention center during the trial proceedings and the time spent there would count to whatever time she might receive if found guilty.

He then asked if the prosecution had anything to add. The lawyer that represented the IRS said there was nothing to add.

Maite was handcuffed and led out of the courtroom and was taken to a transport van that would take her to San Antonio.

Brian and Kekoa went to the airfield where their chartered jet was waiting for them. They were leaving in the early evening and would arrive in Maui the morning of the same day.

Brian looked at Kekoa and asked what he thought about their gun battle trials in the field. Kekoa shook his head and replied that he felt like a gunfighter in the wild west. He went on to say that he was going to try the blind fold test to see if he could match his boss.

Chapter 11: Family

It had been a very trying week. Brian was happy to be going home. Given the multiple gun battles they had encountered, he was thankful that neither he nor Kekoa had been injured. They had been involved in more gun battles than he had envisioned but their gun range practices, and their use of the Kevlar vest had given them a huge advantage. The fact that both had become dead shots and were able to react rapidly in the field had also made a tremendous difference.

He and Kekoa spent quite a bit of time discussing the change that the trip had made on both. They agreed that some luck had helped but both agreed that deep analysis of the situation, good planning and a cautious approach had been key. They also agreed that even with all of that they still had to be ready to use the gun handling skill they had developed.

They both hoped that Maite would drop her threat about retribution, but they would keep track of her. Currently she was very angry and still seeking revenge. He was not sure if time would make a difference. She faced a solid ten years before she would be able to ask to be released for good behavior.

This case had gotten them much more personally involved with the target billionaire than the earlier cases. It had become very personal when Maite decided to have one of them killed. She had tried but failed four times.

Brian spend a long time talking to Annie as he began the flight back to Maui. She let him know that she was relieved and ready to have him stay in Maui for a while.

He decided to stretch out and sleep for the rest of the flight. The private charter landed in the early morning hours and went to a position that allowed Kekoa and he to walk directly into the luggage handling area.

They were surprised to be greeted by Annie, Linda, and Laurie. After hugs and kisses Annie led the way to the long-term parking area.

They decided to drive across the Island and have breakfast at their favorite mom and pop restaurant.

During breakfast, Brian was asked about the details of arresting Maite and turning her over to the IRS. He decided to make the story an adventurous and exciting tale.

He started the story on Maui on the day of the luncheon where Maite had tried to kill him the first time. He embellished the confrontation and had Maite threatening to kill him during the lunch discussion between them. He then inflated Kekoa's action of saving him from getting shot as they were walking to the car. He said that he had randomly fired at the gunman that had shot at him and was later surprised that he had hit him.

He said that the car had raced out of the parking lot and got away because he was too slow in trying to stop them.

He recounted the fact that he went to Mexico where he met up with Eduardo who was the equivalent to a DEA agent. They then had gone to check out the house that Maite had purchased in the Yucatan peninsula. As he walked carelessly along the beach, he was hit in the chest by a bullet fired by gunman who worked for Maite. He had responded, and his random shot had apparently hit the gunman and mortally wounded him. He was worried about facing the second gunman and decided to hightail it off the beach and get out of the area.

Eduardo skillfully ensured the escape and took him to a grand estate where he met a person who was Alex's friend.

He asked if anyone might know who he had met.

Both Linda and Laurie shouted out, "Wow!" he got to meet the "Angel on the Hill."

He nodded and said that he slept at her home for one night and then Eduardo took over and helped him get on his way back to Maui.

He then went on and described the assassination attempt that took place, again on Maui, a few days later. He described how he became the decoy who carelessly wandered around on the veranda and gave the assassin the opportunity to shoot him.

Luckily, Leilani and her team had stepped in and killed the assassin.

The assassin had died in a hail of bullets but not before he had also shot Leilani in the chest. He added that both had been saved by the Kevlar vests that they were each wearing.

He looked at Linda and Laurie and asked who they knew wore the same vest. They both laughed and replied that it would be Aunt Alex. He nodded and said that he had followed her advice and everyone who worked around him had a Kevlar vest and outfit because of her.

He went on with his story and shared the fact that Kekoa, his wizard partner, had been able to track Maite to St Barthélemy a small island three hundred miles east of the Dominican Republic and a third of the way around the world from Maui.

On the way there, they had stopped in Mexico City where Kekoa, he and Eduardo, their Mexican DEA friend had met up and were out at dinner when a pickup with a fifty-caliber machine gun mounted on it came around the corner and began to shoot. He pointed at Kekoa and said that he had returned the gunfire and because of his lightning-fast reaction and his excellent shooting had killed the shooters and disabled the truck before they did any harm.

The three of them decided that they were not welcome in Mexico City and left early the next morning to St. Barthelemy.

He added that they stayed at his beach front home there and enjoyed a few days on the beach before going to Maite's home and arresting her and getting on a flight to Mexico.

Lead by Kekoa who led the way through a hail of gunfire they got her to the plane. He pointed to Kekoa and said that his shooting skills were far beyond his own.

On the way back while Eduardo worked at convincing Maite to sign an agreement that stated she was entering the US voluntarily, Kekoa found out that the plane was being tracked and that Maite had sent out an emergency signal from her phone. He figured that an ambush was planned and recommended that upon landing the plane should be diverted from its normal unloading position to one where they could safely get Maite to a van that would take her and the rest of them to the border.

Because of Kekoa's foresight they all got safely across the border, Maite was charged and would go to trial in San Antonio.

Brian smiled and finished his story with, "Then we came home to be with the most beautiful women in the world."

Laurie gave a small laugh and asked what he was doing while Kekoa was taking such heroic actions.

Kekoa spoke up and said that if they inserted Brian's name into all the heroic actions that Brian was giving him credit for, they would have a more accurate telling of the story.

Annie pulled Brian to her and gave him a kiss and said that she did not realize what a humble partner she had.

Linda asked if he had identified the next billionaire that he would go after.

Brian smiled and said that Kekoa, though great in the field was very slow at finding the next target billionaire. He added that it did not matter because what he had his mind set on was a family vacation at their new house in St. Barthelemy.

Annie smiled and said that she had been thinking about a cruise from Seatle to Anchorage Alaska but a family vacation to the Caribbean was more enticing. It would allow her to continue to work on her tan.

Linda and Laurie chimed in that they were ready to go immediately.

Kekoa smiled and said that if they stretched the vacation out for a month, it would give him time to work on the billionaire list to determine which one Brian should target next.

Brian looked at Annie and asked if a couple of days on the beaches of Cabo San Lucas, a few days in Cancun, a few days in Jamaica and the remaining time in St. Barthelemy sounded like a good itinerary.

Annie, Linda, and Laurie all chimed in and said that it sounded like a true family vacation.

They left two days later.

Kekoa spend each day communicating with Eduardo and following the Maite's prosecution. She had kept her originally assigned lawyer but had augmented her defense with additional lawyers.

Her defense was very weak because the evidence against her was overwhelming. She ended up getting four consecutive guilty verdicts. Each verdict was a five-year sentence that was to run sequentially. She faced twenty years in prison.

The IRS was recouping taxes on close to four billion dollars. Including the penalty for paying taxes late, they recouped six hundred million dollars. One hundred eighty million dollars was awarded to Brian.

He and Brian had discussed what they should do with the billions that remained under Maite's control. They had agreed that they should leave several million dollars for her but that the remainder should be moved to a trust fund that would provide money to Mexican charities. Additionally, the home in Barthelemy would be made available for vacation stays to the factory workers in the factories she owned at no cost.

Kekoa closed the three offshore accounts and set up an account in Mexico City for the trust and moved four million into the bank that Maite used in Corpus Christi. He wondered what her reaction would be when she learned that she was no longer a billionaire.

He informed Brian that the money had been reallocated.

Brian responded with a well done and a thumbs up and, "on to the next one."

The End

About the Author

Ronald E. Mueller
remwriter95@gmail.com

Ron grew up in what is now Flint River State Park in Southeast Iowa. The 170-year-old house Ron lived in is built into a hillside. It faces a 125-foot-high cliff towering over the little Flint River. The house and the land talked to him about; the passing of time, the struggle to conquer the land, the struggles people faced and the wonder of nature.

He climbed the cliffs, crawled into the caves, dove from the swimming rock, collected clams from the bottom of the pond, gigged and skinned frogs for their legs. He trapped muskrats for fur, hunted raccoons in the dead of night, and with only a stick hunted rabbits in the dead of winter.

His young life was outdoors, and nature tested him.

He walked to a one room stone schoolhouse uphill both ways. A stern but warm-hearted teacher, Mrs. Henry was instrumental in shaping his character as she shepherded him from the fourth to the eighth grade. A Montessori before its time. It was a great way to grow up.

His experiences inter-twined with snippets of fantasy lend themselves to the adventures he leads the reader through.

Ron Mueller

Published by: Around the World Publishing LLC.